THE SWAMPS

THE SWAMPS

SERAPHINA NOVA GLASS

Podium

Cover design by Elizabeth Yaffe

ISBN: 979-8-3470-0444-7

Published in 2026 by Podium Publishing
www.podiumentertainment.com

THE SWAMPS

CHAPTER ONE

Macy

The cypress trees look like finger bones with the flesh stripped off, and the fog feels alive, electric with something—maybe just the ear-ringing buzz of insects in the swamps, but something else too, something unsettling and eerie.

"Ethan!" I shout when I see it, but he can't hear. He's inside, unpacking our supplies. We took a ratty wooden boat from the mainland and rowed across the glossy swamp water to this cabin that was very misrepresented on the Airbnb listing and looks like it hasn't been inhabited in years. We could have driven, but the area really requires four-wheel drive, and Ethan's Corvette would never handle it. I'm already regretting coming here.

Even though pinpricks of anxiety climb my spine and I should just leave it alone and go inside, I stare at the strange objects hanging from a dripping Spanish moss tree at the water's edge. I walk over and gaze up, trying to figure out what I'm looking at. A small leather pouch, a checkered cloth wrapped in a tight bundle, and tiny paper boxes are all suspended by wires and strings tied around the boney branch. A lock of stringy red hair hangs from a long black thread, and a tooth is wrapped in twine. *Are those from a human*, I wonder, disgusted at the thought. It looks like a psychotic baby mobile. I reach up to touch one of the boxes, and when it opens, a splash of blood spills out onto my face and into my open mouth. I scream bloody murder and drop to my knees.

"Jesus Christ!" I spit and gag, desperate to get the vile liquid out of my mouth. The cabin door slams, and hurried footsteps approach.

"Hey." Ethan kneels next to me and puts his arm around my shoulders. His eyes widen when he looks at my face. "Jeez, Mace. Is that blood? What the hell happened?" I can't answer.

"Macy! Hey, look at me. Christ, are you okay?"

I point to the tree, wiping my tongue on the inside of my shirt and repeating "Oh my God" under my breath about a hundred times.

"Oh. Well, shit, babe. You're not supposed to touch it," he says with a smirk. It's gris-gris."

"It's what—what?"

"It's a talisman around here. It's supposed to protect you from a curse—like black magic stuff. You'll see that all over," he says casually, like he's explaining the local wildlife. "Probably don't mess with it next time."

"Are you laughing?" I snap.

"No. I'm not laughing," he says, trying to keep a straight face.

"There is *blood*! In my mouth, Ethan! God!"

"Come on." He puts a hand out to help me up. "It's just old animal blood. You'll be fine."

"Oh, well if that's all," I say.

Inside the cabin, I brush my teeth four times and then crack open a beer, ignoring its spearmint aftertaste. It's room temperature, but the heat is too relentless to be picky, and the AC just makes a knocking sound and dribbles yellow water on the floor. I sit cross-legged in front of a box fan and scroll on my phone, looking for the contact info for the woman who rented us this place, because clearly we can't stay here. The photos online must have been from years ago, before the wood rot and overgrown cross vines that almost swallow the place whole. The counters are a shit brown-colored vinyl, and the floor in the tiny kitchen is chipped linoleum in a hideous yellow floral pattern. It's like going back in time. I had to have Ethan take the deer head off the wall because my vegan heart could not handle looking at it, its dead eyes staring right back at me. The antlers over the fireplace are pushing it. Plus, there's an old shotgun leaning up against the wall like that's normal. Or legal. The only thing I like about the place is the kitschy singing fish on the wall—Big Mouth Billy Bass—that opens its mouth and sings "Take Me to the River." Overall, it's a very unsettling place.

In this small, coastal parish, there is no shortage of ghost stories and tales of curses and evil lurking. People here still lay stacks of nickels and paper flowers in front of Marie Laveau's tomb so she will grant their wishes. We visited her tomb once for an episode of our true crime YouTube channel. The voodoo priestess is thought to grant wishes from beyond the grave. If you ask her for something and you get it, you have to go back and thank her. They don't let people touch her tomb anymore, but that doesn't stop folks from leaving offerings, turning in circles three times, and making X motions to show their gratitude.

Some believe in the old spells of chicken feet warding off evil, graveyard dust—which you can conveniently buy on eBay now—to put a hex on someone, or sprinkling gunpowder in your bathwater for protection against spirits. Voodoo dolls and pins are actually still a thing. It's part of the inherent creepy charm of the area, I suppose.

Ethan is the one from Louisiana and grew up around these swamps, so he's much more accustomed to these local quirks.

When Emily Tremblay went missing a week ago, we both became interested in the story to cover for our channel. We had heard about this place a month earlier when we were filming an episode on the Magnolia Plantation and then realized there was a much bigger story to cover. Everyone around these parts is calling her disappearance a curse, voodoo, black magic.

Our YouTube channel, Ghost Patrol, is focused on paranormal ghost hunting, not real missing people, but we couldn't ignore all the local accounts of an evil presence in this town pointing to this being connected to something beyond your average missing persons case.

We've been in talks with Netflix for a couple months, negotiating a possible season of *Ghost Patrol.* We never thought we'd go from a tiny YouTube channel to having this opportunity, and now that it's being dangled in front of us, Ethan and I both feel like we have a lot to prove with this investigation.

"There's a Hilton seven miles north," I say to Ethan as I walk onto the rickety front deck perched on stilts over the murky water. I flop down on a dusty couch, because of course this place has a couch on the porch to class things up. I look at him as he fiddles with the AC unit sticking out the front window, trying to get it to turn on.

"We can't do that," he says, distracted, turning a rusty metal piece with a wrench and wiping his sweaty forehead with the back of his hand.

"Why not?"

"This place is right where it all happened. Emily was last seen walking home from a restaurant half a mile thataway, and Elizabeth Brockton lives six cabins down the swamp that way. We need to be in the heart of it, not at a Hilton miles away," he says.

Two disappearances. One is everyday news, sadly, but a few weeks after Elizabeth Brockton, Emily went missing just a mile away from where Elizabeth was last seen, under very strange circumstances. Elizabeth had been sitting in a chair at the water's edge of the property where she and her husband lived with their young daughter, right across the water from our cabin, and vanished. No screams or struggle heard. Her car and phone were at home where she had left them. No money has been accessed from her bank or credit cards. No footprints up the muddy embankment to the house that drizzly night. It's like she dissolved into thin air. Same with Emily. Yes, the walk from the Crawfish Hut where she was last seen was a mile from her house, and anything could happen in that stretch of cypress trees and gator-infested water, but the strange thing is that her mother reported that Emily was paranoid and had stopped leaving the house not long before her disappearance. We don't know all the details yet and are trying to get her mother to meet with us, but it's all suspicious.

So Ethan's not wrong; we should be close to the story, but I don't know if I have the stomach to stay. Two women just vanished. I feel the weight of it like a stone in my chest. We may have come for the Netflix deal and fame of cracking this case, but now it's so real. It feels different. Important. Urgent.

When I first heard about Elizabeth, a pain gripped my chest. She has cancer and was given a few months to live, as reported in the paper.

When I was fourteen, my mother died from lymphoma. A couple decades later, I still see her as weighing eighty pounds, curled up in a hospital bed, her neck and chest covered with golf-ball-sized tumors. The lumps looked more like horror movie stage makeup than part of an actual person. It seemed impossible that someone could be that sick and still be living. In an effort to shield me from the trauma of it all, my dad took away my final days with her, not allowing me to visit her in the hospital. I think about Elizabeth's little girl—the small amount of time they had left together on this earth and how it was robbed from her. From them both. What kind of monster would do that?

I can still taste the bitter iron in my mouth from the blood, and it makes me want to scrape my tongue with a butter knife, but nothing helps. I blow the air from my cheeks and pick up a can of bug spray, making an insect-repelling mist around myself before sitting on a red aluminum chair and trying to catch a breeze that doesn't come.

It's dusk, and the sky burns orange above the trees, making them look like they're on fire. A low rumbling starts up, like the cabin is about to take off into space, and I whip my head around.

"Yes!" Ethan shouts, pointing proudly at the AC unit, which has hummed to life.

"Thank God," I say, cracking open another beer from the cooler and handing it to him. He sits in a rocking chair next to me, and we stare out into the dark trees.

There's a crunching sound like feet on twigs maybe. I tense and hold perfectly still, listening.

"Did you hear that?" I ask.

"Could be a Squatch," he says, standing and angling a flashlight across the water and into the junglelike brush. "Just my luck we finally catch a Squatch, and I don't have the camera rolling."

"Please stop saying 'Squatch,'" I say, grabbing the camera, placing it on the tripod, and pressing record. This is our usual drill when any action is sensed: We roll. I stand next to Ethan, my face in the frame as he flashes his light around, commentating.

"Here we are in the spot where Emily and Elizabeth went missing only a few weeks apart," Ethan says over his shoulder to the camera. "Macy heard something out here, and we're checking it out. Not many Sasquatch sightings in this area, sadly. Only thing ya gotta worry about over here is gators."

"And actual potential murderers on the loose, but you know . . ." I add. That's my role—the skeptical cynic who doesn't believe any of this paranormal bullshit. It makes for great on-camera chemistry.

"Tomorrow, our trusty sound guy, Max, will be joining us, so we'll have a better quality update for you then, but we wanted to let you know we're here and lots more to come," he says. The video is garbage. It will be posted to our channel for all the world to see with thirty seconds of nothing to really share besides a distant sound in the trees that could be anything, but content, content, content. That's what people want—an authentic experience with us "in the moment." In the thick of it. A video that will have fifty thousand views by tomorrow. It's a bizarre world we live in, but it's working for us.

"And," Ethan continues, "we'll be interviewing Elizabeth's husband, Shane Brockton, on a live stream tomorrow night, so don't miss it. Details in the show notes." I stop the camera.

"What?" I snap. "You didn't tell me that." I can't mask the smile across my face. This is huge.

"I told you I had a big surprise for ya," he says.

"I thought it was running water and AC?" I ask, and he laughs.

"You said you've camped a bunch of times. This is nothing compared to that."

"I said I *glamped*. Which comes with a rain showerhead, AC, a mint on my pillow, and bottomless cucumber martinis. How did you get an interview with Shane?"

"He wants to find her. He talks to the press a lot, so he's open, and he thinks these types of channels can help get the word out. He said he'd do whatever he can to help bring her home. That means talking to us, I guess."

"Wow. That's . . . amazing."

"It's worth staying here for, right? The AC is on now, and I'll call the landlady to get the water sorted. Maybe she can get someone out here tomorrow."

"I know Max would brave the yellow water and mosquitos and all that, but Tasha is coming with him, so we'll see how that goes." Max and Tasha, who do the sound engineering and editing for our videos, have been good friends of ours for years, and I know her well enough to know she likes turndown service and a good spa as much as I do.

"There's prosecco in the cooler and a hot tub. She'll be fine," he says.

I look over to the very questionable hot tub to the side of the cabin. "Ew."

"I'm gonna post this video and get the camera equipment ready for tomorrow," he says and heads inside.

I sit for a while and take in my eerie surroundings. The symphony of nighttime swamp sounds—croaking, from bullfrogs with their low-pitched drone and narrow-mouthed toads that sound like sheep to the chirping and stridulation of cricket wings electrifying the heavy air. I think of Emily and Elizabeth and wonder if they're out here somewhere. Seems like you could get lost forever if you wandered too far. Is that what happened? It would be so easy to do—one wrong turn and suddenly you've lost your footing. You could die of dehydration, a snakebite, quicksand. Is that a thing? Drowning, heatstroke. Gators—for sure there are gators. Jesus, so many things. I try not to think about Grunch, the cannibalistic creature rumored to roam these swamps. But the thought is there now, and all I can envision is it sucking out my organs.

Ethan and I had talked about starting a true-crime podcast long before we were married and long before we actually started anything serious. It feels like destiny though because even in our early dating years, discussions of serial killer documentaries and *Dateline* episodes punctuated our dinners out or pizza nights in, as did our mutual fascination with wives who poison their husbands with antifreeze and men who murder their wives for the life insurance payouts (and think they won't get caught even though they were dumb enough to update the policy merely days before the murders). This stuff bonded us, but our podcast started slowly.

At first we decided the true crime space was too saturated and we could gain a quicker following by reporting sense-tingling, bizarre stories like the woman whose tongue swelled up so big in her sleep it asphyxiated and killed her. When they lanced her swollen tongue in the autopsy, dozens of maggots swarmed out and spilled onto the steel table, causing the medical examiner to throw up right on top of the body. It was all linked back to an envelope from a thank-you card the woman licked days earlier. Apparently, flies are attracted to the adhesive, and the tiniest little cut from the envelope must have allowed the eggs to hatch inside her tongue. We thought the story was gold, that people would tune in just for the shocking news we brought them each week. We even interviewed the man the thank-you card was sent to. He told us the victim was his coworker and he wished he'd never scraped the snow off her car that day so she wouldn't have had a reason to send that thank-you card, but we only had nine subscribers listen to the podcast episode.

The woman who swallowed her wedding ring during a carjacking so it couldn't be stolen and then was gutted for it anyway, the rat mistakenly baked into a loaf of bread at Deli Rios, the kid from Michigan who bit down on something rubbery in his Arby's roast beef sandwich only to find a partial human finger one of the workers had lost in the bun slicer—no one cared.

So we shifted our focus to ghosts, and what do you know, it worked and grew fast. Ethan the believer and me the eternal skeptic. Apparently, Netflix thinks our opposing views on the topic make the show charming and bingeworthy.

What I won't admit to Ethan though is that it feels wrong. I'm thrilled all this success is happening, and maybe I'm wrong and we can really do some good here, but it seems so out of our jurisdiction. This is not the Island of the Dolls or Lizzy Borden's house where she was suspected of murdering her parents over a century ago. This is real women currently in danger, and it gives me a knot in the pit of my stomach.

Maybe it can be good for us too. Sometimes I feel like I'm losing him to his work. The late nights shooting footage, poring over video clips, obsessing over getting every detail just right. It takes a toll. We bicker over nothing, lose patience with each other all the time. Maybe this deal could take the load off—a whole team of producers and a crew. No more grunt work. Maybe.

Once it's dark, I go inside and we do our nightly routine.

"The gun and car keys and kitchen knives are all accounted for, and the alarm is set," Ethan says, fiddling with the motion sensor alarm he has attached to our bedroom door.

"Did you check everything—under the bed, drawers?"

"Nothing sharp, nothing dangerous."

"Thanks," I say slipping under the patchwork quilt that smells like the inside of an old church. If we don't set that alarm that will howl if the bedroom door is opened, anything could happen. My sleepwalking has caused countless problems over the years. I could stab Ethan in his sleep, thinking he's the monster in my dream; I could take the car and drive into the black swamp water, or just decide to go for a swim with the eels and gators. It's horrifying to think about what I could do, all the close calls that have already happened. So the best way we found to control it is to make sure the alarm sounds if I get up and try to leave the room. It works, but every night, setting the alarm, talking through the checklist, is this constant reminder of my disorder—a reminder I'm not normal and not safe, and I hate it.

I try to sleep, but it's no use. I'm awake for hours, wishing I never came here, thinking about the missing women. How does a person disappear? It's not an image in a news report on a screen anymore. It's a whole person with a vivid, complex life—decades of memories, fears, ambitions—and in an instant, all of it is over. Am I fooling myself, thinking we can really help find them when trained detectives have no leads? Are we doing this for all the wrong reasons? I blow out a deep breath and close my eyes, willing myself to sleep.

Sometime in the small hours of the morning, a sound wakes me up. A knock or a door slamming. I can't tell if I dreamt it or if the sound lives somewhere between sleep and dream. Maybe it was just a tiny creak in the wood of the cabin that only sounded deafening in my twilight state. I'm disoriented. It's dark. But then I'm sure I smell cigarette smoke. I sit up and am paralyzed with fear, too shocked to release the guttural scream rising in my throat.

There is a man standing over our bed. He's holding a hammer. It's Ethan who screams. The alarm he set is wailing, and I'm frozen in place. He scrambles to his feet and grabs for the shotgun leaning in the corner and aims it at the intruder, shrieking, "Get out of here, motherfucker!" But the man doesn't move.

CHAPTER TWO

Tasha

Shacks on stilts, floating marshes, heavy mossy tree branches hanging over algae-painted water that glistens green in the moonlight. It feels like we've traveled to another country down here in these swamps, but impossibly, it's only a few hours from civilization.

Max's Jeep bounces over uneven roads as we make our way to Ethan and Macy's rental before dawn. Why so early? Some bullshit about how banshees and Squatches are nocturnal, if you ask Max, but what he won't say is that he can only afford to take a few days off work for this. Even though they're paying us for sound engineering and editing services, we're not the ones making buckets of money and getting famous, like Macy and Ethan surely are. It's a side gig for us, but I know Max is secretly hoping we get some credit too. A spot on the show, a break of some kind.

No matter how many people ask me if I'm jealous that Macy fell into this when she had a job as a phlebotomist and ghost hunted for fun on the weekend with her then boyfriend turned husband and cohost and is now internet famous when I'm the one who got a master's degree in acting and could do a better job in front of the camera, the answer is of course not. No. I'm fine.

What good would it do to dwell on it? *We must be willing to let go of the life we have planned, so as to have the life that is waiting for us.* Someone said that. E. M. Forster, I think. Words to live by. I'm here to support Macy and Ethan and make a few hundred bucks. I've accepted the shape of my life, and I'm happy for them. That's it.

After all, you're one thing when you go into college and another when you come out. You enter a Broadway-bound theater major and leave prepared for a career as a bank teller, maybe a tech at Jiffy Lube or a nail salon . . . or a real estate agent. I did what everyone else in my cohort did and ended up at an entry-level job completely unrelated to my acting aspirations. I sell new builds in the suburbs of Baton Rouge. This—coming to the bayou to investigate a couple disappearances—is the most interesting thing I've done since Max's and my honeymoon in Niagara Falls a few years ago, so I'm delighted to simply get out of town.

As we bump over the last stretch of muddy dirt path and come to a stop in the first clearing in front of the cabin, I can already see something's not right. The cabin looks nothing like the Airbnb photos they sent, firstly. The wood is weathered and sun bleached, and the roof is metal, rusty. You could get tetanus just by looking at it. If Jed Clampett emerged from the screened-in porch, nobody would bat an eye. I guess I won't hold my breath for a welcome bottle of champagne or a charcuterie board.

"Yikes," Robert says from the back seat.

"I concur," I say.

Macy and Ethan are standing outside, Macy with her arms wrapped around herself and her head down, and Ethan gesticulating, shouting at someone—a figure standing in the shadows on the front porch.

I clutch my coffee cup and jump out. The horizon is streaked with purples and pinks as the sun tries to poke through, and it's just enough light to make out the figure Ethan is talking to. An impossibly small, elderly woman with a shock of ghostly white hair and chilling blue eyes. She stands with one hand on her hip, a cigarette in the other. When we approach, Ethan pauses and gives us a quick "sorry, I'll be with you in a second" gesture as he argues with the tiny smoking woman. Macy comes over and hugs me, then seems to attempt to disappear behind me as we all stand and try to understand what's going on.

"We knocked several times," the old woman says. "Edgar works the graveyard. I told ya! He has to do repairs when he gets off work between four and six a.m. What's the problem?" she asks.

"Who's Edgar?" I whisper to Macy.

"Handyman. As it turns out," she whispers back. We haven't seen eye to eye on most things the last year or two. Drifted apart I guess you could say, and it's probably me—the stress and all the tension in my garbage pail of a life as of recent, but as we share a smirk at Alma's giant Tweety Bird T-shirt with its cigarette holes and her braless boobs hanging down to her knees, I remember why we're friends. It's those stupid little moments. We turn our attention back to the argument.

"The problem is, you can't have a guy come into our fucking room at five a.m., holding a hammer and making everyone shit themselves. Do I have to explain that?" Ethan says.

"I told ya. It's in the contract. If you call in a maintenance request, expect the technician—Edgar—to come the next morning between four and six. Did you even read it? We knocked. It's my property, isn't it? I can come in anytime I like. If you guys wanna sleep all day instead of answering the door, that's not my problem." With this, she crushes her cigarette out on her shoe and flicks the butt into the murky water under the cabin stilts. "And don't touch the damn gun. Who said you could use it?" she adds. We're all quiet.

"Well?" she says, waiting for an answer.

"Sorry, ma'am," Ethan says.

"We appreciate you taking care of the water, Alma. Thank you," Macy says, giving Ethan a look to drop it. Alma, I guess her name is, shakes her head and turns on her heels to walk inside holding a small toolbox, leaving us standing under a canopy of cypress trees, dumbfounded.

"She showed up in your room at five a.m.? Jesus. I woulda shit myself too," Max says. Before we do the obligatory round of hello hugs and ready ourselves to listen to the whole story, I clock the moment they see we have an extra person in tow.

"Uh, hey, guys," Ethan finally says, giving Max a half handshake, half back slap and looking at Robert without saying anything more.

"This is my brother, Robert," Max says. "You met once at a Super Bowl thing a while back. He was scheduled to stay with us for a visit, so when you called about this, we thought . . . the more the merrier." He tries to say this as light and airy as he can muster. Max tried to get rid of

Robert, to reschedule his brother's annual visit from Des Moines. He didn't want to miss this potential opportunity with all its possibilities, but Ethan decided pretty last minute he needed a small crew, and Robert had already bought his ticket. Max thought it was better to show up with him than have Ethan say he'd find another sound guy.

"Right, nice to see you, man," Ethan says, and I can't tell whether he's annoyed or not. "The accommodations are . . . a little subpar, but we'll manage."

"Oh, take a pill!" Alma calls back to us as she enters the cabin. Macy breaks a smile at this, a little bit of color returning to her face.

"There's a video game called *Escape the Horror House*," Robert says. "It looks like the cabin in that—the one where they find all the severed heads."

I close my eyes and take a deep breath. I don't look at Macy and Ethan. It'll be fine. Totally fine.

"The AC comes and goes, and the water is yellow, but we have gallon jugs," Macy says. "Apparently, the man who gave us a fucking heart attack is in there working on it. Let's get your stuff inside."

We pull backpacks and totes out of the back of the Jeep and haul everything inside. A very large, middle-aged man with ruddy cheeks and a bald patch at the crown of his head is bent over, crack visible to all, doing something under the kitchen sink. The place is smaller than I thought. A ratty bearskin rug covers part of the wood plank floors in the main room, and there's a plaid couch against one wall. Mismatched chairs surround a kitchen table painted white, and the yellow kitchen appliances look like they're from the 1970s. There are only two bedrooms, both with a log bed frame and patchwork quilt draped over it.

"I don't mind the couch," Robert says. I'm glad he said something normal because he can come off as an oddball. I know him better, so I can overlook the awkwardness, but I'd like to get this started off on the right foot and not have him offer up any nerd facts about Dungeons & Dragons or cosplay just yet. He's a big ghost hunting enthusiast, so he was thrilled to come, but it's better if they don't catch on to his weirdness until we're knee-deep in this thing and it's too late to send him packing.

Macy collects some mugs from the cabinet and offers coffee as we sit scattered around the small space—Ethan perched on the arm of the couch, Robert cross-legged on the floor, because of course he is, and Max tinkering with the camera equipment while Macy and I sit at the table where Alma has lit another cigarette and is tapping ash into a Santa Claus ashtray.

Nobody says anything. We're trapped, waiting for Edgar to finish doing whatever the hell he's doing.

"It's a corroded pipe. He'll have it fixed in a jiff," Alma says in her raspy smoker's voice. "This is why I don't rent to teenagers. You don't read the rules in the contract." She pulls out a can of Dr Pepper from a pocket of her big denim skirt and snaps the top open.

"I'm almost forty, ma'am," Ethan says. He does not add any complaints about the false advertising she used on this shithole, which I think shows restraint, probably because there's not much we can do about it and we just want to get working. And we certainly can't complain since we surprised Ethan and Macy with an extra person.

"Is Edgar your son?" Macy asks, tying to fill the uncomfortable silence. Alma barks out a laugh that turns into a short coughing fit before she replies.

"Does it look like somethin' that big came outta this vagina? No way. One day I started noticing weird stuff at my place—damp towels in the hamper I didn't put there, extra plates in the dishwasher, a couple boxes of Rice-A-Roni missing from the cupboard. Then one day I hear something funny out in the shed. I go down and see a hot plate and a sleeping bag, and don't ya know, Edgar was living in there for three months, helping himself to my amenities when I was gone during the day and sleeping there at night."

"Jesus," Max says, looking over at Edgar, who's still half under the sink.

"So I gave him a job. He was down on his luck, and I needed a handyman. Win-win," she says, gulping down her Dr Pepper. The five of us exchange glances.

"You weren't worried he'd murder you or anything?" Robert says.

"Goddamnit, Robert," I mutter under my breath.

"Naw," she answers, like it was a perfectly normal question. "I mean, if he wanted to kill me, he had a lot of opportunity while he was lurking around my house at night while I was sleeping, right?"

"That's true," Robert says matter-of-factly. Macy's eyes are frozen wide, like a deer in headlights, trying to take in the strangeness all at once.

"Now stop yappin' and let him finish his work in peace," Alma says, slurping her Dr Pepper and smacking her lips.

"I'm gonna check out this beautiful campus," I say, pushing open the screen door. I wander around the side of the cabin and hear something slither from the overgrown brush and into the water. It gives me chills. There's a toilet sitting on its side in some tall weeds, some rusted car parts, and a stained mattress just for whatever reason dumped behind our luxury accommodations. I look at the two sheds on the property that look like they might fall over and poke my head inside one that looks like a hoarder may be trapped under the garbage inside. Delightful. Why I am here?

I wander back to the front, hoping I have missed most of the staring-while-waiting-for-Edgar-to-finish awkwardness, and thankfully, I see Alma standing in the screen doorframe, giving a lecture.

"Since you didn't read the contract, you better know the rules. No drugs. I don't need anyone drowning in the hot tub, do I? No loud music. No pets. The cleaning and laundry is done each Saturday. Don't touch the washer yourself. Just leave the clothes in the hamper. Also, don't go in the sheds, for God's sake. There are two sheds on the property. One that used to be an outhouse. When the toilet hole filled up, they sealed it—boarded it up. The other one is tools and none of your business. There's a full list of rules tacked by the front door. Read 'em. Got it?" she asks.

Huh. I wonder why she doesn't want us in there. All I saw were an old propane tank, plastic bags filled with plastic bags, a rusted ladder, a wheelbarrow that looked like it was from the 1800s, clay pots, hubcaps, and a pile of shitty rusted bikes. And an Easy-Bake Oven from the 1970s that belonged in a horror movie. But there *was* something interesting: ammo. In a small cardboard box under the workbench. I made a special mental note about that. Just in case things get . . . even weirder and we need that gun we aren't supposed to touch.

"Got it, ma'am," Ethan says.

"I can read you kids if you want. I live across the swamp in Cabin 23. Come on by later."

"Read us?" I ask.

"Your fortune. Tarot cards. I got a little shop in the front room. Twenty bucks. Ten for you causa the yellow water."

"Oh," Macy says, and then it's silent again.

"Do you have a crystal ball?" Robert asks. Ethan is staring at Max with a "who the hell is this guy" expression on his face, but Max is deliberately not looking back.

"Yeah. The ball, the cards, pendulums, the whole nine," she says.

"Crystal balls have been used since 3000 BC. Did you know that?" Robert asks. Alma blows a puff of smoke at him.

"Ya don't say."

"I had a Magic 8 Ball once, but it's not the same thing," he continues. "If you can tell the future, how come you can't tell what happened to those two missing women," he asks, and everyone looks in unison at Alma, who blows out another puff of smoke and raises her eyebrows at him.

"Did I say I could read the past? I said fortunes. Are they here? With us? Can I read their palms or cards? No. That's not how it works. What the hell do you know about the two missing women? You're not even from here."

"Theresa Caputo helped solve a murder. Why can't you?" Robert says.

"Who the hell is Theresa Caputo?" Alma snaps, increasingly irritated at the direction the conversation has taken, but I'm mildly amused at this whole unexpected turn.

"Uh. *Long Island Medium.* There's only fourteen seasons," Robert says flatly.

"Did I say I was a medium? A fortune teller is not the same thing as a medium. Listen," she says, standing and pushing in her chair with a piercing squeak. "We don't like outsiders meddling in local business around here." She looks over to Edgar, who's standing upright now and wiping the rust from his hands on a kitchen towel.

"Come on, Edgar," she says as he collects his tools. She turns back to us. "Mind your business . . . or you'll be sorry."

"Is that . . . like a threat?" Max asks.

"It's a warning."

With that, Alma suffers another short coughing burst. Edgar tips his head to us and exits the cabin door. She starts to follow behind but then stops and looks at us.

"None of you are safe here. I'd get outta here if I were you. Except for you," she says, grabbing me by the wrist so hard it hurts. I gasp and try to pull away from her, but she digs in, holding my wrist even tighter and staring me right in the eye.

"Except for you. You're already dead. You have the curse attached to you. I can see it. Can smell your tongue rotting in your mouth." She drops my arm and walks out the front door.

CHAPTER THREE

Macy

That evening, I tried to calm Tasha down by digging into Alma Braithwaite on the internet. She doesn't have a website, but her shop, which is essentially her front porch decorated in candles and lava lamps and beads and stones and little glass bottles filled with swirls of purplish-brown liquid, is on Yelp. A handful of tourists have left reviews and photos of her setup. I guess a 3.2-star rating isn't bad for a business on the crumbling front porch of a swamp cabin. The only negative review was from a woman angry that Alma wouldn't give her change for a twenty for her fifteen-dollar palm reading.

There's also an article about her in the *Daily Herald* from a few years ago where there's a photo of her holding one of the potions—she calls them herbal tinctures—claiming they can cure everything from psoriasis and anxiety to headaches and indigestion, and unsurprisingly these roots and barks and vinegars smashed up into smelly liquids and gels can also lift a curse. "Of course Madame Alma is just trying to set up a sale for a hundred-dollar curse tonic," I tell Tasha, but she's still shaken. I would be too if I'm honest.

After a day of shooting B-roll in the areas Emily and Elizabeth were last seen and interviewing some of the willing locals off the street outside Willy's Diner where we ate lunch, we stocked up on food and beer from Dupre's Value Mart. The cabin was supposed to be fully stocked for our five-night stay. It's stocked all right, but with Bartles & Jaymes wine coolers and Keebler elf cookies and not much else besides some canned soup, expired soy sauce, and a few rolls of paper towels. I'm annoyed, but Ethan loves it. Can't get enough of the absolute gold each bizarre new thing we encounter seems to be.

Currently, he's filming the exorbitant number of E.L. Fudge cookies stacked up on the inside of the pantry and cracking up while Robert is in the background discussing how the Keebler elves started in the 1960s and there are eighteen elves in all and they are likely supposed to be middle-aged in the ads. Max is drinking a room temperature watermelon wine cooler and snort-laughing along with Ethan, but Tash and I aren't as amused.

I thought I was about to have my skull bashed in by a Neanderthal wielding a framing hammer upon waking, and

Tash was told she was gonna die, essentially. I think both of us might want out of this whole thing, but I said I would at least do the Brockton interview. Shane said he'd see us after work. I want to talk to him; it's important. It's always the husband after all, right? That's a terrible thing to think since I never met him, but it's a fact.

I tell the guys we should get going, and everyone agrees, so I go to the porch to sit in front of the box fan and wait for them to get ready and gather their things. It's nearly dusk, and I've been watching for Tasha to wake up from a nap, but it's getting late and we don't want Shane to have a reason to say no once we get there. I try to memorize the questions I want to ask him so the interview doesn't seem stiff or rehearsed. Not for the first time, I think Tasha would be better at this than me. I get nervous speaking in front of a camera, but she's a natural. I don't tell her that.

I hear a flurry of shuffling feet and voices inside, but only Max emerges.

"She doesn't want to go," he says.

"That's okay. Probably better to keep it small anyway so the guy is more comfortable. Let her sleep," I say.

"I should probably . . ." He gestures inside, indicating he should stay, and since she'd probably behead him for leaving her alone in a creepy swamp cabin. I agree.

"Robert is probably better than me with the sound anyway," he says. Max does a good job of talking up his brother and not letting Robert's uniqueness be a reason people shit on him. I appreciate that.

"Totally fine," I say with a smile.

A few minutes later, it's Ethan and me, along with almost-complete-stranger Robert, climbing into the low-country boat we rented for the week and pushing out into the murky green water to the Brockton house. Shane lives in one of the areas you can only get to by boat, which seemed exotic and worth the great footage we'd get even a couple hours ago, but now . . .

The minute we start floating away from the dock, I wished to God we had left earlier. The enveloping darkness and the still, black water, from where a gator could emerge at any given moment, is only a small part of my growing anxiety. Having my skull crushed into powder by a gator's strong bite or my flesh stripped off in bloody ribbons seems improbable. Whatever happened out here to Emily and Elizabeth, that's what I fear more.

A mist hovers above the water's surface as we float through duckweed and cottonwood and listen as the swamp comes alive around us with humming cicadas, the clicks of Cajun chorus frogs that sound like cracking bones, and the lonely call of a barred owl echoing through the dense night air. I shudder a little despite the oppressive heat, and none of us speak until we finally reach Brockton's dock, tether the boat to the mooring line, and carefully carry our camera equipment up the grassy embankment to Shane's house. It's nicer than expected, certainly nicer than our shithole of a cabin. I guess the other side of the swamp is like the other side of the tracks, the trailer homes and teetering bayou cabins giving way to something resembling desirable single-family homes. Modest still, but not in the scary category anymore.

"You sure you're good to go?" Ethan says to Robert as we approach Brockton's door. I know Ethan well enough to understand he wants to ask him to please not interject or have an opinion or ask any questions, or speak at all really, but he also doesn't want to be a prick, and most things can be edited out of footage, so he does not say any of that.

"Well, I was DP for three television commercials, so maybe you're the ones who should make sure you're good to go."

"Touché," Ethan responds. There is a flat, matter-of-fact way Robert delivers his thoughts, and you can tell it's meant to be just that: a fact, not an attitude. I smile at him in acknowledgment of his impressive credentials, and then suddenly the front door swings open and we're greeted by a little girl with wild red hair in footy pajamas. She blinks at us.

"Is your dad home?" I ask, but she doesn't move or call for him.

"Are you Lila by any chance?" We only know her name because one of the papers did a story on Shane's terminally ill wife and how her disappearance has traumatized their child, Lila. Ethan hands over a bag of E.L. Fudge cookies we brought specifically to win her over. She looks up at us, then grabs the bag and runs, dissolving into the shadowy hallway.

"Okay, then," Ethan says. I push the door open a few inches with my index finger and say, "Knock-knock," and then I jump, hand to pounding heart, as a large, sandy-haired man seems to materialize out of nowhere behind us, not, in fact, from inside the house.

"You're the YouTube people," he says as more of a statement than a question.

"We are," Ethan says.

"I'm out back, working the fire up. You can talk to me there," he says, and we follow him back to the water's edge at the bottom of his property where he has a fire going in a pit. He must have been in the shed or somewhere else for us to have missed him on our way up. I can already tell Ethan is liking this—an interview in front of a blazing fire with a backdrop of night swamp. Not on stools at someone's sterile, fluorescent-lit kitchen island.

While Ethan and Robert set up lights, the small girl comes down, her feet now bare and chocolate smeared around her mouth, and she sits right next to me on a log bench. My instinct is to move away from her, but I don't do that. She takes my hand with her sticky fingers and holds it but doesn't look at me. She watches her father poke the fire while the guys finish setting up, and I feel a deep ache for this unknowable little person who lost her mother, a pain I know all too well. And who, according to the article, hasn't spoken a word since.

I think of my own mother and how she still occupies every corner of my mind. She is every memory and every comfort—baking pumpkin seeds on cookie sheets, and growing basil in the windowsill, and crafts on rainy days. She is kickball and Easter dresses and catching June bugs in jars on summer nights. And if Lila hadn't lost her mother to the swamp or to some murderer, or to whatever has happened, she would lose her to cancer soon anyway and would still be robbed of all of that. The weight of this feels too heavy to hold right now. I'm not cut out for this "real people" thing. Again, the overwhelming feeling washes over me. *I want to go home.*

Ethan sits across from Shane in an Adirondack chair while Robert stands behind the camera. Ethan smiles at Shane. He tries to seem inviting and friendly, but we all know how strange and bizarre this is.

"Thanks for talking to us," he says, and Shane nods. I think about the photo of Elizabeth that's been circulating in the press where she's holding a plate of lopsided cupcakes and laughing in a turquoise sundress, and I have to resist the urge to cry, reminding myself I'm a professional now.

Shane looks like he's been crying for years and years. The creases below his eyes are dark and exaggerated, and there is no light in his eyes. He doesn't offer us anything to drink or make small talk, or even inquire about our names. He perches at the edge of his seat and asks what we need to know.

"Sir, do you mind if I record this? We get more responses to our stories with video."

"Sure, whatever, but I don't know what else I can tell you that I haven't told the police," he says, picking at his cuticles.

"We have a unique audience," I say softly. "People watch the news passively and think 'Oh, that's terrible that happened,' but our listeners are armchair detectives. They want to help, so all the information we can give them could get us closer to finding Elizabeth."

Shane sighs and nods.

"Well, I'm still a suspect, let's get that out of the way, but when they finally drop that nonsense, maybe we can find the real guy. She's sick, you know. Of course you know that part." He doesn't wait for a response. He cracks open a can of Coors and pokes at the fire some more. Lila has left my side and gone to stand next to her father, patting his arm sympathetically in the flickering firelight, and then she falls to the ground and begins making snow angels in the grass.

Ethan looks to Robert and gives a subtle nod to make sure he's getting footage of the girl while trying not to let Shane see. The last thing we need is for him to feel exploited, but it feels a little like that's exactly what we're doing in his vulnerable state.

Shane continues, "So she was sitting out with a cup of tea down there—the edge of the water." He gestures toward where we pulled up our boat. "She likes to do that in the evening. Sometimes she falls asleep. When she didn't come in by the time I was getting ready for bed, uh . . . like probably ten p.m., I went out to get her, and she was gone. That's all I know. It's not much. But that's it."

"This was on the fifth," Ethan asks. Shane nods. We already know the basic details. It's been thirty-four days since her disappearance. Shane reported to the paper that he has little hope for her return given her fragile condition. He can't imagine she's survived this long without her medication. We know her cell phone was left on the chair she was sitting on, and there has been no credit card activity, but I want to hear it directly from him. He changes the subject.

"Did you talk to that moron Levi Churnock?"

Ethan shakes his head.

"He hangs around the church revival tent in town and tries riling everyone up with his conspiracy theories. Elizabeth was spending time with him—listening to all the garbage he was saying. He was brainwashing her. And they wanna suspect me. He's who they should be talking to . . ."

"I'm sorry. Can you repeat his n—" I start to say, but before I can finish my sentence, I feel a dog licking the palm of my hand under the bench. When I look down, I jerk my hand away. It's not a dog. It's the girl. She looks up at me with an unsettling smirk and bites down as hard as she can on my wrist.

"Holy shit!" I leap to my feet, but she's latched on to me.

"Lila Sue, get on out of here," Shane bellows, standing and pulling the little girl up by her ear as her jaw remains clamped firmly onto my wrist. He grabs the girl around the waist and tries to pull her off me. She screams in protest once her jaw releases from my flesh, and then she grabs for my hair.

"Lila, goddamnit!" he says. He turns to us apologetically. She pulls away from him and scurries up the grassy embankment and into the house.

"Sorry 'bout that. She was struggling before her mom went"—he stops himself and sits—"and now she's just . . ." He makes a descending whistling sound.

"It's okay," I lie, because we need this interview to continue. I hold my wrist and try to ignore the puncture wounds on my skin so we can just wrap this up and get the hell out of here. I sit back down.

"I didn't know she was struggling before," Ethan probes.

"Oh, yeah, she's, you know." He points to his head, making a twisty gesture with his index finger. "Sorry again. I hope she didn't hurt you," he says, seemingly ready for us to leave.

A crashing sound, like cracking glass, punctures the air. All three of us startle and look for the source. Lila is throwing herself at the sliding glass door. She's making a running start and slamming her little body into it until spiderweb cracks appear across the surface and a few drops of blood smear the glass.

"I'm sorry, she's just, she's . . . really not well. I think you should probably go." I can feel Ethan wanting to protest as Robert covertly turns the camera to capture the event.

"Yes, of course," I say before he can speak. As far as footage goes, we have more than we expected, and there is not much else we'll get out of a man who only repeats that he knows nothing. Robert chucks the tripod over his shoulder and Ethan stands. I nod at him and we quietly make our way down the bank, looking back to see Shane kneeling next to the child and her crying into his shoulder.

What the fuck just happened? I think, but before I can say it, Ethan waves me to get in the boat quickly. He puts his finger to his lips to shoosh me as we clamor in and glide around the corner of the towering reeds out of sight from the house, but with a clear view of his property. Ethan pushes his oar against the muddy bayou floor until we reach the unseeable space where the water moss meets the land. He looks around, making sure nobody is in sight or floating in a nearby boat before he speaks.

"We can't leave yet," he says. "He's the main suspect."

"He didn't say *main* suspect, he—" I try to correct.

"We have to get some video, watch him awhile," he says.

Robert echoes my thought from earlier. "Most homicide victims die at the hands of their romantic partners, so it's probably him," he says, and gives a "Robert has spoken" expression to back him up. So as much as I'd kill for a lukewarm Bartles & Jaymes and a lumpy bed at the moment, I shrug in passive agreement and sigh. He's right. We should stay.

We soundlessly dip our waders into the dark water until they meet soft earth and pull the boat as quietly as we can through spider lilies and cattails up onto the embankment. We crouch down and make our way up the side of his property. A rusted toolshed sits only thirty feet or so from the water's edge, and we hide behind it, positioning ourselves so we have a view of the back door of the house and also the lot that stretches from the door to the water. There is an archaic-looking swing set up near the house and a dead vegetable garden, but we are keeping an eye on the fire pit where Shane has returned and is now sitting in a camping chair with his head cradled in his hands. The girl is nowhere in sight.

After forty-five minutes of sitting against the shed on damp grass, I pull out a can of insect spray and aim it at a cluster of gnats that have formed a cloud around my head. It's all I can do to not run directly up to the main road and find a motel. I spray and wave vigorously, and Ethan gives me an exaggerated, mouth-gaping look because of the spray sound I'm making. The camera on his phone is on, and he's aiming it around, whispering commentary into it about the suspect having a suspicious-looking van parked out front—the kind with no windows that kidnappers use—and that he's acting off and his child is feral. I mean, in all fairness, who wouldn't be acting off in this situation? When he aims the camera on me and my bug spray, I hold my middle finger up and smile.

“My colleague, ladies and gentlemen. Very mature,” he narrates for the video, then turns it off and gives me a look.

“I think it’s time to go. I’m getting eaten alive. He’s not doing anything. He’s fucking crying, Ethan. This feels wrong. What do you expect here? You want him to walk out and confess?” I whisper, but I’m impatient, and my whisper has an edge.

Then I see Robert’s eyes widen—a sort of “holy shit” look on his face. He turns his phone camera to Shane, who is standing. He runs a hand through his hair and flicks tears from his eyes. He looks back to the house as he lights a cigarette. He kicks at the stack of wood inside the round brick surround of the fire pit and lets out a guttural scream that makes all of us leap. I cup my mouth with both hands so I don’t scream myself.

Shane picks up a half-squashed metal can of lighter fluid and douses the wood with it, and after a few long pulls on his cigarette, he tosses it onto the wood where it bursts into flames. Ethan and Robert are both filming this on their phones as if they’re watching a movie and the best part is coming up where we witness the murderer disposing of the body, but in reality, it’s just a guy lighting his fire pit, probably to let his scary kid roast marshmallows or do something happy to distract from her unthinkable loss.

But then, In the flickering glow of the fire, I see Shane's eyes dart around. He looks in our direction—directly at the shed. Holy crap. He sees us. He must see us. Robert pockets his phone and looks like he'll make a run for it. Ethan keeps his camera rolling but shrinks and backs up, looking to the boat, judging the distance it will take us to run.

Shane is now walking determinedly right toward us. We all freeze, but he stops dead. He doesn't see us. He pushes in the door of the shed. The old aluminum door catches on the ground, but he forces it open, cursing, giving it a little kick, and then he goes inside. We sit so still and quiet I can hear myself blink. A few moments later, he's pulling an enormous, fifty-gallon stockpot, dragging it toward the fire pit.

Ethan army crawls to the side of the shed for a better view. Robert is right behind him. I reluctantly follow, even though this is madness and I look like I'm in a boot camp obstacle course, elbows and belly to earth, inching my way through mud in the darkness. By the time I get myself around the side of the shed and look, Shane Brockton has the pot on a metal grate over the fire and is filling it up with water from the garden hose. I didn't know they even made a pot that big. It was almost as big as me. What was it for? Shane stands, smoking, holding the hose. A lowball glass of what looks like scotch sits on the arm of one of the chairs, collecting beads of sweat in the humid night air. He wipes his forehead with the back of his arm and positions the hose so it stays put, filling the pot on its own, and he goes and sits in an old, torn web-strap lawn chair that looks like it won't hold him. He sips on his drink and watches with an unreadable expression.

Ethan looks back at me with wide eyes. I give him an encouraging nod to keep filming. Shane stands and turns the hose off as he pulls the snakelike end of it out of the pot and tosses it to the ground. His head turns toward us again. Ethan turns off the camera and ducks. I grip his hand, thinking we're screwed for sure this time. Best-case scenario, I'm about to spend the night in a police station. Getting murdered is looking more likely. But again, no. He walks back to the shed, and we hear a low grunting come from inside. I can feel the vibration of it through the thin tin walls and up my back as the heaving and grunting continue. I can't afford to even turn my head to look at Ethan because I can't risk the potential sound it could make. We remain paralyzed in fear, and after a few moments, Shane is pulling a black garbage bag across the yard. It's full and clearly heavy because he's struggling.

A wave of nausea rises in my throat. I know it can't be what it looks like and we are just wound up and looking to see what we want to see, but there is a smell that is not my imagination, and I think I really might vomit. It's like Ethan can sense it because he gives me another gesture to be still. Robert is wide-eyed and terrified. Are we all thinking the same thing?

Shane lets go of the bag when he reaches the fire pit. With a swift jerking movement and a loud grunt, he hoists the bag up to his chest and gets a hold around it, his face reddening with the effort, and he dumps the contents into the boiling water.

A flash of pink flesh can be seen in the space between the opening of the bag and the top of the pot as the contents fall in. It's unmistakably skin—an arm, pale skin. I scream, but not because this deranged man has just dumped a body into scalding water to cook it, but because of a high-pitched buzzing sound that has come out of nowhere. The little girl appears in the doorway of the shed. She's holding a drill. In the muted glow of starlight, I can see her tangle of wild hair. She is aiming it at us, the sharp drill bit spinning, as she lunges toward us. Now Ethan is screaming. We scramble to our feet and start to run back into the reeds to escape her. Robert is clambering, crawling across the grass as we try to get to the safety of our boat. Ethan stops and tries to pull out his phone and get footage even as he's moving backward away from her.

"Run!" I yell to Ethan, infuriated he's trying to capture this instead of getting to safety.

"Who's there?!" Shane yells when he hears us. I can no longer see the girl, but I hear the drill getting closer to us, somewhere hidden in the reeds. She's behind us, running at us. Shane's voice gets closer, but I can't turn to see him because we just have to get out. I hear an animalistic howl. I don't register right away where it's coming from, but then I see Ethan fall to his knees. He's clutching his shoulder and moaning. A pair of green eyes blinks at me, a glint of moonlight illuminating them for a brief moment, before the child is gone, the reeds rustling in her wake as she runs away.

"What the fuck?" Ethan screams, a jagged drill bit protruding from his shoulder. He grabs at it, cutting his hands on the sharp grooves as he tries to pull it out of his flesh.

"No!" I yell. "Don't touch it. Go, go!" Robert puts his arm around Ethan's shoulder and helps him down as we all rush desperately to the boat, scramble inside, and push away from the shore. We glide into the black water as Ethan holds his hand over his bleeding wound, howling in pain. Shane is standing on the bank, staring out at us, a mixture of shock and fury in his eyes. He doesn't say a word.

We continue staring silently until we float out of sight, behind a wall of Phragmites and Typha plants along the shoreline.

Then with a shocking bang, Ethan falls to the bottom of the boat, unconscious, blood blooming through his pale shirt. We are miles from help.

CHAPTER FOUR

Tasha

We're waiting in the emergency room, drinking tepid coffee when two police officers arrive at the triage desk asking for Robert Hawthorne. Robert leaps up and goes over to talk to them. They move to the space on the other side of the front sliding doors, and Max and I stare but can't hear what they're saying.

"Are they pressing charges against a traumatized six-year-old?" I ask. Max raises his eyebrows but doesn't respond. He keeps his focus on the police, and we both wonder what the hell Robert could be saying to them. What the hell happened over at that house?

Robert gave us the basics about Ethan's injury but has been pretty quiet since we arrived, and I haven't seen Macy or Ethan yet. I only know he had a drill bit embedded in his shoulder and passed out and that Robert called an ambulance from one of the docks across the swamp and waited for it at the cabin of some stranger who tried to help. I know the little girl was taken in for a psych eval because she was out of control, but that's the extent of it.

After a few minutes, I hear the officers ask about Ethan Goff, and then they disappear down the hall.

"Well, that's a relief," Robert says as he returns to the row of plastic chairs where we're sitting. The color is back in his face, and he looks like a different person from the one who was sitting here five minutes before. He opens a Twix bar Max got from the vending machine, sits down with a sigh, and takes a bite.

"What's a relief exactly?" Max asks.

"It was a pig boil."

Max and I exchange a look of bewilderment even though Robert saying weird shit isn't new.

"Brockton. The guy we interviewed. We thought he was cooking his dead wife in a crawfish pot." We both blink at him without saying anything. What is there to say to this nonsensical sentence he just uttered?

"The police went by. It was a pig. I guess there is a big church revival set up in town, and folks volunteer to bring dishes for fellowship after the sermon. That's what the cop said. It was pulled pork, it turns out, and not in fact Elizabeth Brockton. We should go to the church, by the way."

It takes both of us a moment to shake off what he's just said.

"The church. Why?" I say.

"Brockton mentioned a guy named Levi Churnock. He was easy to look up with a name like that, so I searched him on socials. He's very active. He hangs out outside the church tent, handing out pamphlets about—from what I can tell—a prison that shut down and let all the inmates free, blaming them for all the scary shit that's been happening around here. But the pastor is telling everyone it's evil and voodoo, and so Levi loiters around trying to educate people. There's this whole weird rivalry."

"Well shit," Max says.

"Yeah, and I guess Elizabeth was hanging out with this Levi guy. She was on Team Prison, it sounds like."

"Good work, bro," Max says, and Robert looks pleased with himself as he pulls the second Twix bar out of the foil and tosses the empty wrapper toward the garbage, missing by a mile. Max puts his arm around me and asks if I'm okay. I don't say that I hate it here and desperately want to go home and that I really resent that we need the stupid few hundred bucks we're getting paid to be here.

"Yep," I say instead, and we all sit and wait in silence.

When Ethan is released, we learn that although Robert made it sound like he'd lose an arm, Ethan only has a bandage and is sent packing with a painkiller and advice to rest. But when we fill him in on Levi and the prison and the revival tent, the five of us immediately head down to the church.

It's just shy of ten p.m. when we pull into a dusty dirt lot between the Crab Shack and a Chevron and see the massive tent in the grassy clearing behind. It's a sight to behold: a big-top circus style covering with poles anchoring it to the ground and metal folding chairs set up in rows. It looks like two hundred people or more are there, fanning themselves in the dripping Louisiana humidity despite the late hour. The pastor's voice can be heard a football field away.

"We're here tonight, friends, to get filled up with the holy spirit! Those whom God wishes to pardon must first see what their sin deserved, and how terrible it would've been if they'd been punished. Only then can they perceive how merciful God has been!"

I exchange a look with Macy and take a deep breath and blow it out hard, preparing myself for the fire and brimstone.

Max grabs the camera equipment from the back of the Jeep, but Ethan shakes his head, indicating for him to leave the big camera behind, which is exactly what I was thinking. That's a lawsuit waiting to happen unless we have hundreds of waivers for all those people to sign, agreeing to be exploited on YouTube. We all know the rub; the only way to do this is to sneak footage on our phones and not draw attention to ourselves. We can blur faces and edit later, but we don't need any nutjob flinging our boom mic into the swamp and punching Ethan in the neck. It's happened before—minus the swamp, that is.

We take in the scene before us for a moment. It's not every day you see a southern church tent revival. I didn't know these existed anymore. It seems very Billy Graham or Oral Roberts circa the 1950s, but apparently these gatherings are alive and well and just as much the spectacle you'd imagine them to be.

We learned from the church website that everyone brings a dish to share. One family will volunteer to bring the main course, and everyone else is supposed to bring a simple offering, so we arranged a plate of leftover E.L. Fudge cookies that I grabbed from the hatch before we make our way toward the echoing voice of Pastor Ken Lawson reverberating through the night air.

A low grumble of thunder rolls in the distance, and heavy gray clouds hang low across the sky. The smell of damp earth and incoming rain clings to my skin as we walk across the stretch of grass and into the back of the tent. A woman in a long skirt and black Hokas nods to us as I put the plate of cookies on the fold-out table next to dozens of other plates filled with Swedish meatballs, turkey pinwheels, and various dips, and she gestures to a few empty chairs in the back row where we then obediently sit.

The five of us exchange glances. I suppress a smirk and see Macy also balling a fist over her mouth to mask a giggle. Because it feels very surreal—like a movie set almost—this pastor behind the pulpit actually pulling out his handkerchief to dab the dripping sweat from his forehead as he sways and carefully crafts the cadence of his words, the rise and fall of his singsong voice seemingly hypnotizing everyone.

A frail woman stands on shaky legs in front of him. He has one hand on her shoulder and the other palm open to God as he shouts into the microphone, distorting the sound when he pops a consonant too hard.

"Lord, I ask you to heal Sister Kathy and her affliction, oh God. I command no more pain. I call on you, Jesus, to work through me and let this woman walk once more, in the name of Jesus." Macy makes a small snort-laugh, and Ethan elbows her gently and gives her a look to keep it together. Then she glances over at me, and we both have to look down to keep from catching the giggles. Not because anything is funny. It's actually quite scary—the congregation weeping with their eyes closed and holding their hands up to God, swaying, mumbling prayers or speaking in tongues or I don't know what, but the absurdity of it all is what makes us uncomfortable.

Just then, Kathy collapses and falls backward. A man—her husband, perhaps—catches her and lays her on the floor. She convulses for a moment as her husband wails. It really is an Oscar-worthy performance.

"Are you healed, Sister?" the pastor asks, and she begins trying to stand, her wheelchair undoubtedly strategically placed on the other side of the tent. Her husband helps her up, and then she's walking, on her own, tiny unsteady steps. Kathy cries and nods. Her husband gathers her up in his arms, and the congregation erupts. They sing and pray and hold hands, shouting to God, crying out. One woman faints, but then, no. She's just been moved by the Lord, and some of the others crowd around her and lay hands on her as she shakes and writhes and then falls still.

I think about the curse Alma said is attached to me. Were those her words? I'm "already dead"? It's so stupid. I mean, of course it is. I'm not proud of the fact that I looked up "how to lift a curse" after that encounter with her. I also don't know who has ready access to mugwort and wormwood to bathe in, as one site suggests. I could burn a bay leaf or find a black candle to light at the next full moon, but the easiest way to break a curse is by cleansing your spirit, praying, they say. I really can't even believe I have let these thoughts go this far. I guess that's what fear does.

The strongest curse is the one we inflict upon ourselves with our own fears. I don't remember who wrote that, but as things become more unsettling, this quote may be the only thing keeping me from actually going down the aisle tonight to repent or whatever I'm supposed to do to get saved. It's all getting under my skin.

Movement to my right shakes me out of my head. Ethan is holding his phone sideways, chest level, trying to remain inconspicuous as he captures the drama on camera. Not exactly ethical, but Max does the same, panning around the crowd while Ethan keeps his fixed on Pastor Lawson. I don't know what I was expecting from this investigation, but this seems criminal—the way everyone is rapt, convinced that evil has a grip on this town and they are all victims. We did our research before we came here, and it wasn't just the two missing women but a series of other odd things that has everyone so convinced of evil interference—the cumulative effect, I guess. Most recently, a teenager named Richy Walberg was found lying in the locker room shower, foaming at the mouth and convulsing. If his teammates or the coach didn't spend so much time panicking because they thought he was possessed by the Devil and needed an exorcism, they might have saved his life since it was, in fact, a fentanyl overdose. Isn't this really a version of that?

The sky around us flickers white as a distant lightning bolt illuminates the sky. I see the faces of some of the crowd in that brief flash, distorted and anguished. This isn't right. None of this.

The pastor gestures for a couple men standing on the periphery, deacons I gather, to escort the "Kathy Show" offstage, then he leans both hands heavily on the pulpit and lets a few lingering moments of silence pass as everyone quiets down. He pats his forehead again with his handkerchief and shakes his head.

In his heavy Louisiana accent, he begins the next part of his sermon.

"There are people living among us, maybe right in this room, who are part of the occult. Evil, sorcery, black magic! In Revelation 18:23, Jesus warns that He will destroy Babylon. He tells them 'All nations were deceived by your sorcery. By your magic spell, all the nations were led astray.' God certainly condemns sorcery, black magic, witchcraft, and anything associated with it, and He will severely punish those who persist in it." Murmured Amens and Praise Jesuses float throughout the crowd.

I think about these words. Babylon symbolizes a corrupt system and the idea of people being deceived by magic spells. As I look around, the irony is not lost on me.

"We're under spiritual attack, folks. There have been holes torn in the fabric of this town, and it's left room for the Devil to get in. Tragedy has befallen our community, and people are scared. I keep getting asked over and over 'What's happening, Pastor? There's evil in this town, Pastor.' And I respond to you, friends, for the wage of sin is death. If we walk in willful disobedience, we are 'breaking covenant,' and that leaves holes for the enemy to bring a curse on us. Brothers and sisters, we are now a playground for the Devil. There are holes for the enemy—for the Devil to get in. Stand with me."

Some of the congregation rise to their feet. A small elderly woman begins playing the organ, and the sound is so unexpected, it jolts the rest of us to our feet, giving me a near heart attack. I meet Ethan's eye and point a few rows in front of us to where a collection plate is being quietly passed around, people placing tens and twenties inside. Ethan catches it on video and then shuts his camera off when it gets to our row. I feel eyes on us. The long-skirted, athletic-shoed woman who showed us to our seats is suddenly there at the end of the row. Ethan pockets his phone, and Macy pulls a crumpled ten-dollar bill from her purse and puts it into the plate before handing it to the strange skirt woman.

Macy looks at me and gulps, then draws her eyes back to the front of the room like we're back in elementary school, afraid of being punished.

"If we want to cleanse this town, we must cleanse our hearts. I invite you to pray with me." Pastor Lawson closes his eyes and holds his hands up.

"Dear Lord Jesus, forgive us our sins," he says, his voice breaking. "Walk on down the aisle now, folks, I invite you. If you need to be saved, or if you've been a backsliding Christian and need to tell Jesus 'I belong to you, I don't belong to the Devil anymore, Lord,' then come on down. Let the congregation lay hands on you, and let's cast the Devil out. Let's make you clean again."

With this, I jab Max with a finger and raise my eyebrows at him, giving him a "let's go" look. With dozens of people filing down the aisle, whimpering or shouting out "Praise be to Gods," it's a good time to slip out. I make eye contact with Macy, and she nods and stands, all of us practically running back to the car, far enough away from the tent to not be heard yelling "Holy shit" and "What the fuck," but we don't get a chance to properly unpack what we've just witnessed because Macy stops and points across the lot.

Breathless, we stop short of the Jeep and look to see a small folding table set up on the sidewalk next to the Crab Shack, in front of Larry's Liquor. At first I think it's someone selling Girl Scout cookies, but given the late hour, probably not. Then I recognize the man from the photos Robert showed us. Levi Churnock.

"Let's talk to him," Ethan says, leading the way. Levi is chatting to a couple who are looking down at a pamphlet in their hands. He's explaining to them that they can scan a QR code and donate to help fight for a good cause—spreading awareness about people like Pastor Lawson preying on people's fear. Robert picks up some of the literature on the table, and Levi glances over as he finishes chatting with the couple, who obviously just want to get back to their car with their bottle of Jack Daniel's and be left in peace.

He approaches us, and I pick up a pamphlet too and page through it.

"Welcome. Hello," Levi says. He's a tall, very thin man with a sharp, angular jaw. He's wearing a baggy muscle shirt and cargo shorts that hang from his wiry frame.

"Whatchya sellin'?" Max asks.

"Oh, I'm not selling anything. I'm here as a public service. But you can choose to donate if you like."

"What's the service?" Ethan asks.

"Well," Levi starts, but Ethan stops him.

"Is it okay if we get you on camera? So your message can reach more people. We can put it on our social media and help you spread the word."

"Oh, of course. That would be great," he says, taken aback. His own Instagram page had nineteen followers, so I can see why this would excite him. Ethan takes out his phone, taps open the camera app, and starts recording. Levi's mannerisms change, like he's trying to "act" a little for the camera.

"I'm just out here today sharing a message that could help save lives. The church is trying to tell you evil abounds. People are scared and confused, and that's when the offering plate comes around, but it's not evil," he says. I decide not to interject by asking how a QR code to get donations is different from an offering plate. "There is a real human threat to our town," he continues.

"I heard you were friendly with Elizabeth Brockton and that you think there are prisoners running loose or something?" Macy says, and I have to give her some credit. So she's learned over their time in the spotlight to ask questions in a way that puts someone in defense mode without saying anything offensive, I'll give her that, but it comes off a little forced. I could still do better.

He furrows his brow for a moment but quickly remembers he's being recorded and regains composure.

"Elizabeth was someone who believed the church was stirring up fear ever since they started to divide the town—an us-against-them mentality."

"Who's them?" I ask.

Macy shoots me an irritated look and pointedly repeats the question. "Who's them?"

He pauses and then answers flatly. "Anyone who isn't us, I suppose."

"And she was involved with your . . . movement?" Ethan asks.

"Yes, but it wasn't a prison. It used to be Avalon Glade Lunatic Asylum. They changed the name."

I look through the pamphlet. Avalon Glade was an institution located ten miles east of town, and with a grisly past. There's a series of graphic photos, and I almost have to look away. People locked in cages, lobotomized with icepicks, chained to things. There's a photo of a guy who was presumably strapped down so long to his bed, his skin had grown over the leather. Overcrowding and profound abuse was widely reported. People were left to starve to death in their rooms. I feel a wave of nausea rising in my stomach. I put the pamphlet down and walk a few steps away, taking a deep breath.

"If there are escaped inmates, how hasn't this made national news?" Ethan asks. "It's not like it's a Squatch. These people must have been spotted if they're running around kidnapping and poisoning people for sport."

I look at Macy, and we both roll our eyes. Because of course he wedges Sasquatch into the conversation. It's amazing how he can do that. And slightly annoying.

"Again," Levi says, "not a prison. I believe there are some very troubled, unmedicated people living among us. I come from a place of mercy and wanting to help."

A deafening crack of thunder pierces the air, and we all jump. We hear gasps from the revival tent across the clearing too.

"Jesus!" Macy says, holding her heart. Fat raindrops begin to fall, and in seconds it's coming down in torrents. Macy starts running to the car with Robert close behind. Levi quickly shoves his precious pamphlets into his pocket and begins breaking down his table.

"Can people go to this asylum still?" Ethan yells over the driving rain.

"Not legally," Levi says before darting off to the safety of the Crab Shack awning.

"Great, let's go," Ethan says.

CHAPTER FIVE

Macy

But first, we sleep. It took some doing to convince Ethan that he needed rest, that exploring an abandoned asylum is best done in the daytime, and that we'd never even find the damn place in the pitch black. Finally, it was decided that we'd go back to the cabin and find it the next day. Ethan did have a good point though. I mean, the video footage we'd get in the middle of the night would sell better probably, but no effing way.

Now it's dawn, and I sit by myself on the front porch with a cup of coffee, watching warm streaks of pink light filtering through the trees and reflecting off the water. I see the eyes of an alligator sliding across the glossy surface of the water and shudder. I will never get used to that—swamp squirrels, as I've come to think of them. I'm from the Midwest originally, and that's how they are down here. Just as everyday as seeing squirrels scurrying up trees—with one deadly difference. Ethan is the one who grew up around here, but even he gets a flash of fear in his eyes when he sees one unexpectedly or they come too close. He's the big shot who chases ghosts though, so he'd never admit he's terrified of them, but he doesn't fool me.

Tasha joins me on the porch with her coffee, and I hear the rest of the crew awake and shuffling around inside, the gurgle of the coffee maker as Ethan puts on another pot, and the sound of static on the television as Max relentlessly tries to get a sports channel to come in.

"He should call Alma to fix it," I tell Tasha as she sits in front of the box fan. It's already dripping with humidity.

"Hard pass," she says.

"Did you get any sleep?" I ask.

"I would have, but Max came up with some theories in the middle of the night and was up scrolling his phone and showing me shit." She lies flat on the wood of the deck and closes her eyes. Max comes out with a sleeve of E.L. Fudge and, as if on cue, launches in.

"Y'all! Search the name Alma Braithwaite," he says, sitting in the deck chair across from me and shoving cookies into his mouth.

"Morning, Max," I say.

"Yeah, morning. For real. Search that name." I do and don't find anything besides an obituary from a few years ago, a photo of a nurse in Kansas City who looks to be in her thirties, and a couple reviews for the fortune-teller business owned by the Alma we know that we already saw.

"What? There's nothing to see," I say.

"Exactly. Levi's handout says all these ill people were let out of the institution. Makes sense they wouldn't have a searchable past if they were institutionalized their whole life."

"Max thinks anyone who's not on Insta doesn't exist," Tasha says.

"No. I really looked. There are a handful of search engines that can find anyone. She's not on any of them. Sure, she materialized with this cabin and little front-porch-creepy-palm-reading thing, but where was she before that? What if she's like—I mean, you met her—an escapee?"

"Jesus," Tasha mutters.

"I like that idea better than evil spirits," I say.

"And fucking Edgar. That guy escaped from somewhere for sure," he says. Tasha uses her arm to cover her eyes against the sun that's beginning to blaze in sideways, and Ethan flies past us, already loading gear into the Jeep and telling us to "chip-chop-chip because we're leaving in five."

"He read that *Ghost Hunters* filmed at this hospital a few years ago, and we didn't even know it existed. He's a little charged up," I say, standing and gathering my things to go.

As we drive over bumpy backroads to find the place, Robert reads facts about the hospital from the back seat, trying to keep his phone steady with each dip in the road.

"The name changed from Lunatic Asylum to Insane Hospital in 1902."

Tasha snorts. "Like that's any better."

"I think we should use Lunatic Asylum in the footage," Ethan says, keeping his eyes on the precarious road.

"There's an old map of the property online," Robert says. "Infirmaries, staff dormitories, and a work farm. Oof."

"Work farms were actually not the worst thing. Instead of the residents being idle or lying in beds all day, it was supposed to be therapeutic. Growing crops, raising cows—it gave them meaningful things to do," Tasha says. We all turn and stare at her. Max puts his arm around her.

"That's what happens when you get too many master's degrees, folks," he says, and she rolls her eyes at him.

"There's no evidence at all they let the remaining residents simply walk out free after it closed down. They were probably relocated, and this is a little silly," she adds.

"Actually, it's possible," Robert says. "There was a deinstitutionalization movement, and people were just . . . let out. But the last patients were there in the nineties. So the unstable people Levi is blaming would have to have been roaming town for decades. Doesn't add up." He continues to swipe his finger up the screen of his phone to continue his research.

I know this matters little to our story. The sensation of getting video footage in a place like this and the duel between satanic evil versus human evil is really more than we bargained for when we came to track down two missing women. Do people really even want the truth if the truth is less interesting?

When we find the place, we drive down a long cement driveway with weeds sprouting through the cracks to access the buildings. The eerie brick buildings are still standing but are shrouded in overgrowth and show decades of neglect. They look almost like they're bleeding; the peeling paint, rust, and crumbling brick make it look like they're rotting in the sun. The graffiti is the first thing I zone in on. I don't know why I hadn't thought about others trespassing here—squatters maybe. It's not a bad place to seek shelter, assuming you can find it.

There are dozens of headstones scattered behind the building, buried in the prairie grass. We read about them. They each have only a number carved into the stone—an attempt at honoring the hundreds of patients who were anonymously buried in shallow graves—their remains washed away in flood waters long ago.

We stand in awe as we squint against the sun at the broad, brick exterior of the main building with its boarded-up windows and stony courtyard. The stark towers jutting from the roof and arched windows look like they belong in a gothic novel.

"Fuck," Max says, eating the last cookie from the sleeve and shoving the wrapper in his pocket. He pitches a tall camera tripod over his shoulder and gazes up at the weird bell tower on the main building.

"So, what are you expecting to find here, exactly?" Tasha asks. "The patients from forty years ago hanging out in their old rooms?"

"We don't expect anything," I say, grabbing a shoulder mount rig from the back of the Jeep and handing it to Ethan. "It's just a great place for a short segment."

"Are you kidding?" Ethan says, pulling down the rest of the gear and roller cases and heading toward the building with childlike wonder. "When *Ghost Hunters* filmed here, they heard disembodied voices in the halls and unexplained footsteps. This is gonna be sick."

"I thought they heard that on every episode?" Tasha says, following behind. I see Max give her a little reprimanding shake of his head, and she shrugs.

Without hesitation, Ethan walks up the stone front steps, pulls a crowbar from his bag, and starts to pry the boards off the small window next to the front door.

"Um . . . so like, what about breaking and entering? I thought we were just gonna shoot from outside—just have this for background?" Robert says. I don't even need to look at Ethan to know it annoyed him that Robert used the word *we* like he's part of the crew. He already suspects Robert is here to piggyback on the popularity of our web series, and it takes him some restraint to answer in a measured tone.

"We have an assistant, Janey," Ethan says, "in New Orleans."

"They called the city this morning, who said a guy named Benny Thibodcaux bought the land five years ago—some rich guy who plans to convert the main building into a mansion or something and raise sugarcane on the rest. We thought we'd need to wait to get a permit, but Janey got in touch with Benny this morning, and he loved the idea of his property being on a show and told us to help ourselves. It's all in writing."

Max shakes his head and points at Ethan. "These guys are next-level for a reason, I tell ya. Let's fucking go!" He grabs the board Ethan loosened and starts ripping the rest off like a Neanderthal.

"All right, then," Robert says as Max squeezes through the hole they created and unlocks the front door where the rest of us enter. The place doesn't disappoint. It's frozen in time. Every wall looks like someone has scratched and clawed at it for years—gashes ripped open exposing the old red paint color beneath the gray shreds. Peeling paint is the understatement of the century. It literally drips off the walls and is clustered into piles on every inch of the floor. The hallway is one long stretch with small rooms on each side that were likely used for patients.

We always start by clearing the space. As a group. We begin on the top floor, and then split up, half of us going to each side and getting eyes on every room until we meet in the middle and can be certain there are no squatters or anyone in the place that could not only decide to kill us of course, but maybe more importantly, not influence any noises or movements we may be lucky enough to capture on camera.

We walk with quiet reverence through the space. In each patient room there is little left but more than I expected. It's not our first sanatorium. We actually filmed in Waverly Hills recently, and the interior of that place looks like a bone picked clean. No remnants or evidence of the horrors it once held.

Here, in one of the identical small prisonlike rooms, piles of peeled paint are scattered on the floor, and there's a radiator, a small window, and a single metal-framed bed. Some beds have soiled mattresses still in place, others with the metal springs and coils exposed. All with an undeniable smell even after all these years—a sharp, acrid scent of stale urine and mildew.

We end up in the front entrance after we've successfully confirmed the absence of any other presence. Ethan and Robert set up the lights. Tasha sits against the brick wall of the hallway, picking her cuticles and watching while Ethan and I go over what we'll lead with. He's printed out the history of the place, and we each have a role to play on camera, so we look over notes until everything is ready to roll. We didn't film the part last night where Ethan got a drill bit wedged in his shoulder, but we got enough of the lead-up on camera and posted it to YouTube late last night. Patty Hovland, one of the Netflix creative execs we've had chats with, gave the video a thumbs-up. They're noticing. Will it have any bearing on whether or not they greenlight a season—even if we solve the disappearances? Nobody has said that, but we're doing all we can to clinch the deal.

At the entrance to the west-facing hall is a gate made of steel bars, like in a prison. We decide to stand in front of that for effect, where the camera can see down the long, creepy stretch behind us in the right light, and I am officially ready to get this over with.

When Max calls action, Ethan holds up the EMF reader and begins.

"Guys, we're live tonight at Avalon Glade Lunatic Asylum. After what we showed you last night, it was brought to our attention that this place was somewhere we needed to check out. It's rumored that when the hospital closed in 1996, all the remaining patients were released, free to go, to wander out into the woods with no families or loved ones to collect them. There were over forty patients left when they shut it down, so what happened to all those residents?"

"When you say *rumored*, that means exactly how it sounds, right? People chitter-chattering and making an absurd claim that gained traction . . . but might be completely made up," I say.

"There she is, folks, Macy the cynic," Ethan quips, like part of a well-rehearsed scene—because it is. "Well, what we do know is that other ghost hunters who have investigated this place documented moving shadows, cries in the night, and unexplained humming. So, even though the patient records were lost in a fire decades ago, we know there's been ghost activity. Like many state hospitals we've visited, the unthinkable happened within these walls, and it's not a surprise we'd find spirits trapped here. But what we don't usually deal with is the living. Could there be former patients from this hospital still living out in the swamps?"

"A fire destroying the records seems a little convenient. I don't see any fire damage in the buildings," I say.

"Maybe records were kept somewhere else—the city or county or something," Ethan says.

"Okay, so say your records were kept off campus for whatever mysterious reason—" We start talking over each other.

"Not *my* records—" he says.

"Why would they be kept somewhere else?"

"They probably weren't at the time," he says. But they would have moved the records somewhere after the place closed. The public records I could find only say they were destroyed in a fire."

"Wouldn't they have been digital by then?" I ask.

"Mid-nineties? Probably not."

"Okay, let's go with your theory. Records are lost. You still can't prove severely ill patients were allowed to leave of their own accord—no families to collect them, no money, no help getting back on their feet. Your take is, they wandered out into the distant trees and are living like the girl in *Where the Crawdads Sing*, unnoticed by any locals for a few decades now?"

"It's not a Squatch we're talking about here—"

"If you wedge *Sasquatch* into one more thing, I swear—"

"These folks could be mostly perfectly nice people who have jobs and apartments in town, but the records show this place housed the criminally insane."

"I thought the records were burned in a fire that may or may not be fictional?"

"Some of them. We still know enough about many of the staff and patients from long before that. There were many criminally insane."

"Do you really think we should still be using that term?"

"It's not my term. It's in the records."

"Of course. The records that burned," I say. Out of the corner of my eye, I see Robert smiling, enjoying our back-and-forth.

"One of the long-time residents back in the 1930s," Ethan says, "Roddy Fergus, was committed here because he couldn't stand the sound of whistling, and every time his neighbor, Pat, would water the plants on his apartment balcony, Roddy would ask him to stop whistling. Pat told him to fuck off, and then one day nobody heard Pat whistling ever again."

"Ah, jeez," I interject.

He continues, "It wasn't until months later when the July heat got so bad and there was a power outage that the neighbors started complaining about the smell wafting down into the street from Roddy's balcony. That's when

Pat's body was discovered in Roddy's refrigerator, chopped to bits, kept in trash bags."

"Do you think he really said 'fuck off' if it was the 1930s?" I say.

"I think you've missed the point."

"How did the neighbors he shared a wall with not smell it before then?"

"I told you. There was a power outage that day. They didn't smell it 'cause he was in the fridge . . . until it turned off."

"Fair, fair. So are you suggesting that Roddy Fergus is walking among us still, committing heinous crimes? How old would he be, exactly?"

"No. It's just an example of the sort of people that may have been let go from this hospital. Roddy died in his room in 1947 actually, according to records."

"How?"

"Suicide. He smashed the mirror above the sink and used the glass shards to—"

"Got it. Maybe we can try to have a chat with him and ask him what happened here—where everyone went. What does the EMF show?" I say, looking over his shoulder at the device. Any exciting—" The meter starts to go crazy, flying up past the red zone into the out-of-range mode.

"Whoa." Ethan turns the device to the camera. "For anyone who doesn't know, the EMF reader measures changes in electromagnetic fields. A sudden, unexplained spike in EMF readings is often considered evidence of a potential paranormal presence, so if you—"

I cut him off to keep the drama going because everyone knows what an EMF is. "Okay, Roddy Fergus. If you're here, come have a chat. We have questions."

Bang.

We all scream at the loud noise, and I lurch backward in fear.

"What the fuck was that?!" Tasha has leapt to her feet and is running for the door. The softbox light kit crashes to the ground after Max falls backward into it; near total darkness overtakes us.

"Jesus," I say, frozen in fear. Only the sunlight streaming in through the oversized windows of the front room illuminate the space enough to make out one another's shapes.

Another bang reverberates through the hallway, like metal hitting the floor, followed by a bloodcurdling sound—like steel scraping across polished concrete, as though one of the beds is being dragged across the floor of a resident room behind us.

And that's when I feel it. A hand reaches through the bars behind me—clammy and dirty—and grabs my face. I scream, but it happens so fast that before I can move, the other hand catches me around the neck and squeezes.

The hands feel huge, and I'm overwhelmed by the smell of tobacco. I claw at the hands, but I'm quickly getting lightheaded, and I'm pinned to the bars from behind. I can't move.

Now I feel hot breath next to my ear as they open their mouth and whisper, "Get out," in a tone that chills my blood to the core. A warning.

I try to scream for Ethan, but the hands are cutting off all air, and it comes out garbled. I hear everyone shouting and moving to try to help, but all I see are shadows in the weak glow of sunlight. Someone—Max, I think—is scrambling for the light on his phone. Ethan is screaming. I hear the front door opening.

I claw at the hands pinning me against the bars, but they only press harder around my neck. Then, I feel breath on the side of my face and a tongue lick my cheek. Just when I start to see stars and I'm certain I'm about to lose consciousness, I'm dropped to the floor. I hear footsteps running down the long hallway behind the prison bar gate. I gasp for air as Ethan shines his phone flashlight down the corridor, and we see a hooded figure disappear into the shadows.

373

CHAPTER SIX

Tasha

When I run shrieking out the front doors, I don't know what I expected. The stark contrast between the panicked chaos inside and the peacefulness of the outside is shocking, like when the lights at a bar are turned on just before last call. A moment later, the front doors open and Max yells, "Get him!"

It's so unexpected, it practically gives me a panic attack. In a flash, he and Robert run out, splitting directions and flying around the sides of the building trying to catch the intruder. Or are we the intruders?

Ethan helps Macy to the Jeep and leaves her with me while he grabs the shotgun from the back that he brought from the cabin, which sounds very questionable to me, and then he's off too.

"Jesus," I say, my heart still beating out of my chest as I lock the Jeep doors and look at Macy. She's pale, with a sheen of sweat across her forehead. There's a small red scratch on her neck and bruises in the shape of fingers starting to develop, but nothing alarming that seems to need medical attention.

"Are you okay?"

"I'm done. We're going home." She flicks away a tear. I nod and put my arm around her.

It's a long and silent ride back to the cabin. After the guys spent another thirty minutes searching for the person or the ghost or the former resident and having no luck, they finally gave up. Now Ethan is freaked out that the party is over because Macy repeated more than once that she's not staying and is packing her shit up as soon as we get back.

"Give me until tomorrow morning, Mace. Come on," Ethan says, looking at her in the rearview mirror, her head leaning against the window and bobbing up and down with each bump in the dirt road.

"You can stay," she says. Passive-aggressive, but who can blame her.

"Let me try to get that interview with Emily's family like we said we'd do—remember this isn't a normal ghost hunt. We're actually helping—trying to get answers for these families on this one," he says. She closes her eyes and doesn't respond. Not a bad tactic. I wonder if she'd really go home on her own. Perhaps they'd need someone to fill in. Not that I want her traumatized or anything, but if going home is best for her, I wouldn't try to talk her out of it.

I know the skeptic-versus-the-believer banter is what they do on camera, but the personas have spilled over into real life, and I seem to get along with Ethan better than she does most of the time these days. Maybe it will be a breath of fresh air for people.

When we get back to the cabin, I think we all wish it was the glampy experience we were promised and not a shit pile with lumpy mattresses and the perma-smell of Chef Boyardee hanging in the humid air, but "contentment is one's greatest wealth," I suppose. Who said that? Buddha, I think. He can't be wrong, so . . .

We practically crawl up the rotted stairs like we've just returned from war, when in reality we've been gone three hours. We're all a little traumatized.

"Shut the fuck up," Ethan says, stopping in his tracks, looking down at his phone screen, before Macy can reach the front door and run to her room to pack. Max flops on the porch swing.

"What?"

"No fucking . . . Mace! Our YouTube Live hit a million goddamn views in the last hour. Are you kidding me?!" She perks up and grabs the phone from him to look. Her hand flies to her mouth.

"Right?!" he yells, pumping the air with his fist.

"Holy shit," Robert says, coming around from the Jeep and dropping the gear in a pile.

"Oh my God," Macy says, turning the phone to Ethan to show him an incoming text. "It's from Patty Hovland asking to set up a call for Monday."

"Damnnnn," Max says. I decide to offer a suggestion before Macy changes her mind. Not that I want her to go, but I'm trying to help.

"Looks like you have their attention." Then I look to Ethan. "So seems like no harm if she needs to leave, right? I bet Robert could take you home." Ethan's already asked her if she's really okay five thousand times and if she wants to go to the hospital or anything, and she doesn't.

Ethan ignores me and turns to Macy, a pleading look in his eyes.

Macy lets out a long sigh. "One more night," she says. "But we have to get that Emily interview."

"Yes," Ethan says, kissing her cheek. "We will."

"Awesome," I say. Because what else can I say?

The guys go to town taking more B-roll and asking around, trying to get mini-interviews from locals and push for some ins to get Emily's family to talk to us. Macy doesn't come out of her room, and I don't blame her. I would be pretty shaken too, so I just try to do some work on my laptop and drink a couple of the Bartles & Jaymes from the fridge and wonder how it came to pass that a million people want to see a ghost attack a woman in a mental hospital—because I'm sure everyone believes it was supernatural—and how much money that measly little two seconds of trauma will make them, and how I, on the other hand, showed that dumpster fire of a three-bedroom over on Willow Drive eighteen times last month and if I don't sell something soon, we have to talk about refinancing our house. How?

After a couple of hours of posting the stupid listing all over social media for the millionth time, I go out to the porch and watch the scaly backs of alligators glide through the glassy swamp water and wait for the guys to return. When they do, they come bearing burgers to fire up on the grill and vodka to celebrate the success.

No word about the Emily interview, but Ethan downplays that as he tells Macy, who has emerged from the bedroom, about the thousands more clicks on the video as he makes her a martini. He pours charcoal briquettes into the rusty grill on the porch.

"Hot tub!" I hear Max hoot as he turns on a country station from an app on his phone and holds up a beer, dancing. Robert is taking the cover off the hot tub and poking at the water's temperature.

"It's a thousand degrees," I say.

"Hot tub!" Max shouts again, and I can see they've already had a few in town. Macy takes the drink from Ethan and joins everyone on the porch, looking like she's got a little color back and seems more like herself again.

By ten, everyone is drunk except for Robert, who doesn't care for alcohol or loud music or hot tubs, and has taken his plain veggie burger and whole wheat bun to the sofa doubling as his bed and puts on his headphones to play some video game on his laptop. The rest of the night is utterly predictable for the four of us, so familiar it's nauseating. Ethan and Macy are in the kitchen, and she's crying because she cries every time she has more than two drinks. She's accusing him of embarrassing her by telling some story she didn't want brought up, but I'm not even sure what it is, so I guess no one cared. She then accuses him of being too drunk and of flirting with me. It happens every time. Max is passed out on top of the bed in our room, sideways, with all his clothes and dirty flip-flops still on because he was shooting tequila from some gross bottle they found under the sink. Shocker.

I'm enjoying the hot tub, which is actually pleasant once the sun goes down, and listening to Morgan Wallen singing about sand in his boots, but I am feeling tipsy. More than tipsy, really. I'm at that point in the evening where I regret having that last one and wondering why I even drink at all when I almost never enjoy it.

I hear Macy tell Ethan to fuck off, followed by a door slamming. Ethan comes outside alone, shaking his head. He pops the top off two beer bottles, climbs back into the hot tub, and hands one to me.

"Thanks." I smile, but I don't want it.

It's hard to know who to side with when it comes to the two of them. She has a point. He is too drunk and he can get obnoxious, but when you compare him on the obnoxious meter with Max, not even close. He's a saint compared to Max when he's drunk. Max never directs it at me though. He's just loud and barfs in garbage cans and high-fives strangers. It's embarrassing, but I can overlook it. Maybe because he wasn't always that way. A job layoff and late mortgage payments sort of turned him into that—turned us into something else.

I don't say anything to Ethan as he silently fumes for a few minutes. I'll wait the polite amount of time before I get out of the hot tub and go inside. The music is off, and Max's snoring can be heard through the front screen door but is muffled by the chorus of cicadas and crickets in the reeds and cordgrass around us.

"Welp," I say, ready to leave. The hot water is making my head spin.

"Not you too," he says. "Come on, at least have a night-cap." I pick up the beer and cheers him.

"Yeah, fuck it," I say because I'll be hungover anyway at this point, and I don't really want to go push Max onto the floor and put my earplugs in. And, I like Ethan's company, if I'm honest. It's nice to have someone listen to your whole sentence and not watch the baseball game on the bar TV over your shoulder at a restaurant and say "uh-huh" every now and then, pretending to listen. At least every once in a while.

"Why does she think you're flirting with me?" I ask. "Not that I was eavesdropping, but it's not the first time I've heard that."

"You know how she gets after a couple martinis," he says dismissively.

"Yeah," I say.

"I mean, I think she likes the job security and money that comes with what we're doing, but it's not the dream . . . for her, I mean. But you . . . well I went to film school, you went to art school. You love this stuff. We just have more in common, I think."

"I went to school for theater."

"Oh, what did I say?"

"Art."

"Kinda the same."

"Well, I was in *Alice in Wonderland* in community college, not making bank as an art dealer or selling paintings at a gallery or anything, so not really."

"*Alice in Wonderland*. Huh. Did you play Alice?"

"I did not."

"I bet you were still good though."

"I played the March Hare."

"What the fuck is that?"

"Just . . . shut up," I say, and he holds his hands up in mock surrender.

"I'm just saying, just because I don't know what the fuck a March Hare is doesn't mean we don't share the film, theater stuff, and that's what she seems to bring up after a martini. Anyway . . . don't worry about it."

"I'm not," I say and smirk at him.

"Is that what you think art majors do? Make millions as New York City dealers?"

I laugh and almost blow beer out of my nose. He laughs too and flicks water at me. I flick it back and splash his face, but then I stop in a horrifying realization that I am flirting. I'm acting like a teenager, and it's so cringey I can't even stand myself in this moment. What is wrong with me?

"What?" he asks as I stand to go.

"Nothing," I say, but I'm so intoxicated that I stumble back before I step up to get out, and he has to practically catch me.

"Whoa. It's slippery," he says, and I'm glad he thinks that's all it was. I'm too old to be hammered. I sit next to him on the weird bench submerged in the hot tub water, and we look up at the constellations.

I try to focus on the stars and squint my eyes to make myself sober up and anchor my attention on something. I can only ever find goddamn Orion's Belt and the Big Dipper, and tonight's no exception. I think I see a dipper handle, but that's all.

"The March Hare—is that the queen?" he asks. I burst out laughing, and I don't know if it's all the money stress and rocky shit with Max or the constant state of terror we've all been in since we got here, but I can't stop laughing at this, and tears are falling and I can't breathe and then he's laughing when he realizes how stupid the question was . . . or maybe he still doesn't get it, I don't even know, but then he's just there. Close, skin to skin under the water, and I don't know who moves into whom first, but his hand is on my thigh and we're kissing and he's pulling me on top of him and I'm straddling him and it all happens in a confusing blur of pent-up lust and a haze of alcohol.

Just as it's about to go too far, I thrust my head back, and that's when I see it. A wooden beam above the hot tub with a tiny camera clipped to it—the record button pulsing red.

"Jesus!" I leap off him and scramble out of the hot tub, wrapping a towel around my body and stare up at it. He practically falls out the side of the tub, trying to get out, probably thinking someone else is awake and caught us. But someone has.

I point up at it, silent. He pulls a towel around his shoulders, and we stand underneath the thing, staring, not quite comprehending what's happening. I cup my hand over my mouth.

"Is that your camera?"

"No. Fuck. Of course not."

"Then who? Who just recorded that? Oh my God. Oh my God!"

"Shh. Shh. I don't know. Shit."

A light flips on inside, and we both quickly try to act normal—like we don't even see each other and are just happening past on our way to bed. Inside, Max can still be heard snoring, and Robert is asleep on the couch with his headphones still over his ears, but Macy is standing in the small kitchen, her eyes wide and unblinking.

She's in underwear and a T-shirt, holding a glass of water next to the sink. She just stares at us. But not really at us, more like she's looking past us with a blank, dead look in her eye. Then she slams her glass on the countertop, and it shatters in her hand. Shards of glass and blood drop to the floor, and she screams a terrifying guttural wail.

CHAPTER SEVEN

Macy

The pain wakes me up. I'm standing in the kitchen, staring at my hand, then looking to Ethan and Tasha standing in the front doorframe, wrapped in towels. Ethan rushes to me, but Tasha is staring at me with something like fear in her eyes. That's when I notice the blood.

"Oh God." I start to panic.

"You're okay," I hear Ethan say, but everything feels a bit fuzzy still, and waking up from a deep episode like this takes a minute. He sits me down in a kitchen chair and wraps my hand in a towel while muttering about the first aid kit as cupboards fly open and bang shut.

"You wanna help?" he says to Tasha, who looks like she's in a trance, then sort of shakes it off and moves to help him rummage through the kitchen.

“I’m so sorry,” Tasha says. “Macy. It’s not what it—it was just—” Ethan cuts her off.

“It’s okay. She sleepwalks. She was asleep.” Tasha looks utterly bewildered, but still she leaps into action once Ethan locates the kit and helps him pull the glass from my palm while I look at the ceiling, blinking back tears and wincing. He doesn’t ask me what happened because he knows. I don’t remember anything though. I have gone a few months without an episode and thought maybe I was free of it, but this sets me back, and it’s really the last thing I need right now. Last time it happened, I tried to drive to the Circle K for Nutella, apparently, but Ethan woke up in time to stop me. He has to hide the car keys in different spots at night so it doesn’t happen again.

Tasha’s hands shake as she helps bandage up my hand, and I don’t comprehend why she’s the one shaken. She looks up at Ethan, who gives her a silent little shake of his head, and I can only assume he’s telling her not to start asking about my condition or upset me, but it still seems odd—like they’re sharing some secret, and I remember our fight from earlier. About his flirting with Tasha. I clench my jaw.

“Do we need to go to a hospital or anything?” she asks.

“No, I’m fine. I just need a little space. Go to bed, really—really. I’m good,” I say, trying to arrange my face into something resembling a smile so they don’t worry.

Everything is floaty and staticky after this happens, and I don't want to have people keep asking me if I'm okay. I just like to be left alone.

"Thanks," I say, examining my bandaged hand. I go out to the front porch to get some air. Ethan knows the drill, so he squeezes my shoulder and goes into the bedroom, giving me the space I ask for. Once I'm outside, I hear Tasha tripping over something, stumbling to her room. I've never actually seen her drunk before. She's usually the sober ride or the one-glass girl of the group, but I guess everything here feels strange and off.

I listen to the wind in the trees and close my eyes for a while, waiting out the dizziness and thinking about whether any of this is worth it. It won't make or break this streaming deal, will it? They were interested before. Do we really need to stay in this garbage dump of a cabin and track down clues that should be left for the police to solve?

I think about leaving, but there is something niggling at me—a sense that there is a lot more happening here than the missing women. There were half a million missing women reported last year. Sadly, this is nothing new. What *is* mystifying is the feeling I got when those hands wrapped around my neck. Cold, freakishly strong, appearing out of nowhere, without a sound. And the way they disappeared as quickly after we cleared the place and saw no signs of life there. No car, no footprints in the mud, no sound, no sign of squatters. It takes a lot to get back there—a narrow dirt road and treacherous swamp forest to navigate through, so who would just wander in to attack me? None of that adds up.

Once I'm feeling like all my senses have fully returned, I pull out my phone and do some different research on this town—not the history of the two missing women and Airbnb rental options, but now I actually entertain the stories and factoids Ethan has told me about this place that I only half listened to. It's good for the show to give the history of voodoo and black magic. People eat it up, but I have never believed one single, contrived bit of any ghost, paranormal, voodoo, or magic bullshit that Ethan so passionately subscribes to. But what happened to me in that abandoned hospital needs an explanation, so I let myself entertain the idea, as stupid as I feel doing so, as I google ridiculous and embarrassing searches, because . . . whatever is going on has my attention now.

I type "Avalon Glade occult" and "Avalon Glade dark history." Weird shit starts to populate immediately. In 1988, there was mass hysteria in the town after a young man was found hanging in a tree, spinning counterclockwise. A few months later, his sister was found dead in her bed, her face melted and clothing charred, her left foot severed from her body and resting on the open windowsill, still wearing a pink slipper. There's a photo of blackened, curled toes and scorched toenails against the pastel silk bunny slipper. I almost throw up in my mouth looking at it. Her death is still a mystery. I turn the phone over for a minute and go through a mental list of explanations for this.

Wind could cause a hanging body to spin. Spontaneous human combustion might be a stretch, but it's at least a documented reason for a burning death like that without an alternative.

I read on and see that a few years back there were dozens of reports of locals seeing a shadowy creature said to attack people in the swamps, which led to the deaths of several panicked people who fell from roofs or stairwells while fleeing what they thought was the monster chasing them. No evidence of a monster was ever found.

Mass hysteria. They call it that for a reason. We covered the story of the June bug epidemic in the sixties, when a mysterious disease broke out in a textile factory. The workers experienced numbness, nausea, dizziness, and vomiting. They said there was a bug in the factory that would bite people and make them sick. Suddenly, sixty-two employees developed this mysterious illness; some were hospitalized. After medical experts investigated, no evidence was ever found for a bug that could cause such flu-like symptoms. There was no cause at all.

We also shot an episode covering the soap opera virus, named after the popular teen girl's show *Strawberries with Sugar*. More than three hundred students at over a dozen Portuguese schools reported symptoms mimicking what happened to the characters in a recent episode. The outbreak of rashes, difficulty breathing, and dizziness forced schools to temporarily close. All of it was eventually dismissed as mass hysteria.

Anxiety, panic, frenzy. Of course that's what it is. Still, something feels different about this place, and I can't put my finger on why. A chill runs through me despite the suffocating humidity as I look through photos of all the odd happenings in this town. Birds falling from the sky, graves desecrated, a bloody pitchfork floating in the water. I click a video titled "Avalon Glade Curse" and watch an impossibly thin man sitting in a clearing, covered in mud. Surrounding him are rows and rows of neatly lined up shoes—dozens. He holds his head and rocks in the middle of his shoe rows. Suddenly, he lets out a wail and starts to bury the shoes, each in their own muddy grave. It's so unsettling that it makes sense why the town gets the reputation it has, but I don't get swept up in this sort of thing. I have to remind myself of this.

The further you dig, the clearer the picture becomes. The story behind the dead birds was reported in the *Avalon*

Gazette and features an image of a woman named Linda with a cigarette hanging from her mouth, standing on the precarious stoop of her trailer in an oversized T-shirt that reads MILF across the front, pointing at three dead crows at the water's edge. Although West Nile virus is the most common cause of crow death, this woman, who may or may not be high on meth, says they were raining from the sky. Everyone panics. The video of the shoe man has two hundred thousand views but no source. It has to be staged. Everything has an explanation. All of this can be answered, justified, rationalized.

Before I get off my phone and go to bed, a news story pops up in my notifications. I click on the short video. Holy shit. I stare at the screen, and my hand flies to my heart as I watch the images that fill my screen with horror.

Elizabeth Brockton has been found. Her body. Dead. They aren't giving further details, but there are police and flashing blue lights in the darkness behind the TV reporter. I recognize the spot. There's the tackle shop we passed; I see its faded sign in the background. I have to go. I need to know what happened to her. Oh my God, poor Elizabeth.

I run into the bedroom and shake Ethan. He moans and rolls over. I try again. Shit. They're all hammered. I peek into Tasha and Max's room, and they are both passed out in their clothes on top of the covers. "We're too old for this," I mutter as I fish around in the dark room for my shoes and look for the Jeep keys, bumping into shit and making noise. Robert sleepily sits up on the couch.

"Sorry," I say.

"What are you doing?"

"They found Elizabeth. The police and news are there now. They're . . ." I make a dismissive gesture to the bedrooms to say everyone is useless, and Robert stands and pulls on a ball cap.

"Let's go," he says.

We don't speak on the drive. I was holding out the tiniest spark of hope that she'd be okay and would see her kid again. I think about my mother and the last days I got to see her, the weeping open wounds that never healed, the soiled bandages, the fluid in her lungs. Maybe it was the best thing that could have happened for Lila. She's already so troubled. But still, I would have wanted the chance to say goodbye. I didn't get that, and now neither will she.

As we get closer, a wind picks up, and the accumulating clouds in the night sky blot out the stars, but even through the haze and mist, I see the police barricades and know we have to stay out of sight.

"There." I point to a clearing behind some trees, and Robert pulls in.

I can see her in the distance already, through the thick of trees, her body hanging. Robert sees it too.

"You sure you wanna see this?" he asks, and it's a kindness, but we both know we're all in now. I nod.

"Ready?" I ask, and we move, quietly, careful with our steps. When we get close to the barricades, we stay in the trees behind the police and medical vehicles. We tiptoe around the chaos and the security, staying in the shadows.

"Come on," Robert whispers and points to a patch of willow oaks that we can hide behind with a closer vantage point. My heart is racing. We're so close to the officers on the scene and yet, they don't see us. Could they arrest us for this? Is it illegal to cross police tape if we are technically around it, not through it, and we're harmless?

We pause and stay still when one of the officers seems to turn and look in our direction like he's heard something, but he doesn't see us. Robert touches my shoulder for me to stop once I start moving farther into the trees to get a better look. He taps his ear, and I know he means for me to listen to what they're saying. We crouch down and strain to hear.

"You don't need the coroner to know this poor woman has been dead for a while," one officer says.

"Weeks, at least. Jesus, in this heat. She must have been killed the day she disappeared."

"That's fucked up," the first one says, pulling on latex gloves and disappearing into the darkness as they move in closer to the crew that's working on cutting her down. Robert and I exchange a wide-eyed look.

We continue the twenty or so yards and get as close as we're able before stopping and staring in awe. I can't believe what I'm looking at. No wonder the news isn't showing it.

It's different close up. Elizabeth's body is suspended from the arm of a dead, branchy cypress tree. She sways in the wind by a rope around her neck. I hear Robert gasp. He covers his mouth with his hand.

"Jesus," he whispers. We exchange a horrified glance. A medic arrives in a van, and in the glare of its headlights as it pulls up, I catch a glance of Elizabeth's face too decomposed to make out and her long black hair hanging limp from a broken neck in a gruesome, nightmarish flash I wish I could unsee.

CHAPTER EIGHT

Tasha

My head pounds when I wake up, and I can't believe what I've done. Did she see? I know she was sleepwalking, but who the fuck sleepwalks? I thought it was a joke at first—that she was messing with me and actually saw something and was about to go nuts on both of us, but apparently . . . not. I want to apologize to her profusely, but of course I can't. And what the hell was Ethan thinking? I know what *my* problem is. I'm miserable in general, and Max always seems to be distant and stressed over money, and I've spent all week thinking about whether I need to get a side hustle driving Uber or flipping hamburgers or something to make ends meet. I'm practically middle-aged with a negative bank account balance and a pantry full of ramen and SpaghettiOs. I suck, and maybe having some sort of mental breakdown in the form of almost shagging semi–internet famous Ethan Goff could be forgiven.

It's not an excuse. But pour a bunch of liquor on top of that, and I guess I just lost my mind for a few minutes.

"A man is as unhappy as he has convinced himself he is." I mean, Seneca said that in like 45 AD, and it still holds pretty true today. I'm just saying, I'm very aware this is my fault. What an absolute jackass I am. All I can think about is that camera and who put it there. I have to find out.

When I walk into the kitchen and pour myself a cup of coffee, everyone is already gathered around the coffee table, looking at Macy's phone and talking over one another.

"What'd I miss?" I ask. Ethan goes out of his way not to look at me, probably as mortified as I am, which is fine by me right now.

"They found Elizabeth," Max says.

"What? Oh my God. Wait, like . . . alive?" I sit on the edge of a weathered armchair with a faded mossy-green satin cushion and glance at her phone playing the news story clip.

"No," Ethan says flatly.

"Oh God."

"Rob and Mace drove over there after the story broke on the news," Max says. Robert shows me a garish image on his phone, a body hanging from a distant tree, backlit by headlights. It makes my stomach flip.

"Holy . . ." I shake my head in disbelief. I don't know why I thought she'd turn up—that this was all a wild goose chase for their episode. I didn't think she was really . . . killed. Jesus.

"Her throat was slit, but that was weeks ago. Then she's found like this," Macy says.

"That's bizarre," I say. "Someone wanted her to be found."

"Or something," Max says. I blink at him and bite my tongue at this.

"Emily's mother messaged me back finally, after the news about Elizabeth. She wants to talk," Ethan says.

"Did they know each other—Elizabeth and Emily?" I ask.

Ethan seems pained to have to glance my way, but let's not go out of our way to act awkward *now.* "That's what we have to find out. I still think it's worth going. Mace got a couple shots of the whole scene last night. People online are going nuts. We can get some more answers," he says, and Macy is already up, stuffing supplies into a bag and hoisting it over her shoulder.

"A bunch of folks from town are holding a vigil for her this morning. It's at Brockton's place."

"Is the scary kid gonna be there?"

"She's still being evaluated at the hospital last we heard, but I'm not going there. We decided Emily's mom would respond better to another woman, so Max and Ethan are going to the vigil for interviews, and I'm going to see Mrs. Tremblay. You coming?" Macy asks. Everyone else is now up, gathering water bottles or sunglasses and heading outside. My head pounds, and all I want to do is crawl under the covers and die, but I have something of my own I have to do.

"I'm a little . . . under the weather. I think I'll stay back," I say, desperate to have them all leave so I can try to figure out where the hell that camera is connected to.

"You sure?" Max asks. I clutch my coffee and wave them away. On their way out, Ethan pauses and looks over at the hot tub then subtly back to me. I give an almost imperceptible nod.

"Positive," I say, and then I wait for the sound of the Jeep pulling out of the drive and leap up, rushing outside to see if that camera is still blinking above the hot tub. It's there, but there's no blinking red light on. I am tempted to pull it down and smash it to bits, but it wouldn't matter. It's remotely connected to someone's phone or computer, the data saved there rather than in the camera itself. Someone's watching.

I scour the rest of the cabin for more cameras, looking in all the spots they say perverts might hide a hidden camera—the wall sockets, air filters, smoke detectors—and everywhere in between. There were none in any of those places, but there was one on a shelf in the middle of the living room, aiming down at the common space.

Now that I look again at the hot tub camera, it's not exactly positioned on just the tub, it's sort of mounted at an angle, surveilling the whole porch. Nobody in this cabin seems to know about last night. Macy or Max would win an Academy Award for acting clueless rather than being well on their way to a divorce lawyer if they saw that footage. But what if it was one of them and they haven't looked through the footage? They didn't know what would happen last night. I'm still surprised and ashamed about it myself. Robert has no skin in the game, and the only other possibility is the creepy lady who rented the cabin to us.

I would not put it past her to spy on her renters—perhaps just for sport or maybe to make sure we don't . . . do what exactly? I go inside the front door and look at the list of rules tacked to the wall. *No sidewalk chalk.* Sure, why not. *No music after ten p.m. No alcohol.* Hilarious. *No more than four cats.* Seems reasonable. *Don't sleep on roof.* Hadn't planned on it, but now I'm curious. *Don't use the oven: may explode.* Super.

The list goes on before finishing with a clause that says *Failure to abide by these rules may result in immediate dismissal from the property with no refund.* What if Alma's running a scam? Trying to catch us breaking a rule, which it would be impossible not to do, and kick us out and keep our money? It's the most plausible explanation, but then again . . . where is she? If this *were* the explanation, she'd be here throwing our things on the front porch and booting us out as we speak. Or is she watching us for another reason?

I can't just sit here. I have to do something. I need that footage. It could ruin my life—my already incredibly disappointing and joyless life. Max is a pain in the ass, but I'd never want to hurt him. This is awful. What I did is awful. Alma offered to tell our fortunes, said she has a shop in the front room. That's my way in.

Her house is circled on a small map of the swamps that was in with the rental paperwork. It's on one of the little islands across the way. I get dressed, gather up my things, and take one of the kayaks tied to the dock. I begin to row across the murky black water to see a macabre fortune teller and steal back my sex tape, essentially. Just an average day.

Frogs and slugs and leeches. Fuck me. I take a breath and try not to think about being swallowed up by all the buzzing life around me. The fluttering of beetle wings and clouds of gnats above me, the heartbeats of swamp gators and water snakes watching from where they perch in rotting vegetation, and the curling mist and dripping trees all around me make me wish I could turn around and go home. This isn't a place for people.

Alma's cabin comes into view—clear from the ALMA'S SPIRIT SERVICES sign hand-painted on a piece of cardboard with a moon and star. I glide up through the reeds and tether the kayak to the dock. Her cabin is shrouded in towering sweet gum trees and darkness. On this already cloudy morning with thunder rumbling in the distance, her property looks like permanent nighttime.

From the dock I can see there is a screened-in three-season porch that's completely covered in crap: a pile of damp boxes, old bike parts, dead plants, and a box of Barbie heads. Precious Moments figurines and ceramic unicorns crowd the plastic shelves on every wall. It looks like a garage sale except for a cleared-out spot on one side with a red shag rug, a small card table, and two folding chairs. There's a crystal ball on a lace doily next to an ashtray on the table.

Edgar, the handyman, runs out the side door. He's naked and giggling wildly. He has a house cat under one arm as he hoots and runs around the back of the house. What the hell did I just see?

"Oh, Edgar, you stop it now. Do you want a spank?" I have to try not to laugh and not to vomit at the same time.

It's Alma. She's standing in the side doorframe, shooing him with a broom. She catches a glimpse of me in her peripheral vision and stops cold. I wave, pretending I didn't see a thing, and she quickly disappears back inside. Within a few seconds, she's opening the front screen door and staring me up and down.

"Yeah?" is all she says.

"You offered to read our . . . uh . . . fortunes. I thought I'd—" Before I finish my sentence, she interrupts me.

"Well come on, then; I don't have all day." She lets the screen door slam behind her as she turns and goes to sit at her crystal ball table.

I step inside, and she gestures for me to sit. Honestly, I still haven't shaken off naked Edgar to fully refocus on the moment, so I try very hard to erase the image from my mind, but she brings it up as she lights a cigarette and fixes her hair.

"Edgar gets hot easily. It's the diabetes," she says, shuffling a deck of tarot cards and shoving a long boob back inside her housecoat. I try very hard not to let any expression cross my face.

"Oh," is all I allow myself to say.

"Twenty bucks for the tarot, an extra ten for a palm reading."

"What about the crystal ball?"

"It's out of order," she says.

"Can I use the bathroom first?" I ask, thinking there might be a room in the house filled with electronics and computer screens where I'll see streaming footage of the hot tub and living room at our place right now. Maybe I can pour a glass of water on the motherboard or threaten to turn her in for violating the privacy act or voyeurism or something if she doesn't give me the tape I want.

"No."

"It's urgent," I say.

"Ten-dollar surcharge." I blink at her for a moment and ponder this. It's pathetic that I feel like I can't afford that, but that's my reality. Still. I fish out a crumpled ten from my bag and lay it on the folding table. She pushes the bill into her bra.

"There are only four rooms. I'm sure you'll find it," she says, and when I go inside, my hopes are quickly dashed. The place is tiny and filled to the brim with romance books and newspapers and litter boxes and a Christmas tree even though it's June. There is only the main living space and two small bedrooms off the left side and a bathroom in the back. I peer inside the main bedroom. It consists of a queen-sized bed covered in piles of clothes and open take-out containers and a couple vodka bottles and coke cans.

When I push open the door to the second bedroom, a cat flies past me and I almost fall over backward. The only things inside the room are at least nine cats and a pee-stained mattress in the middle of the floor with food and water bowls scattered about. The window to the outside is open, and it looks like they come and go as they please—like she's created a hotel for them. The whole place is as low-tech as it could possibly be. I don't even see a television or internet router.

Then I remember the shed. The one that Edgar lived in as a squatter before she . . . I guess made him her lover? Okay, I need to get into the shed before I leave. I go back to the porch and sit in the rusted metal chair across from her.

"You met Chuck Woolery," she says.

"Sorry?"

"The cat you let out. What are you snooping around for?"

"Oh, I . . ."

"Don't say ya wasn't," she says.

So I decide to just come out with it. What is there to lose at this point?

"You have a security camera at the rental. You know it's illegal not to disclose that? We could sue you," I say. She crushes out her cigarette in the James Dean ashtray and stares at me. I wish I could take back the words because she looks like she might murder me, and even though she's tiny and I could probably take her, who the fuck knows where Edgar is lurking? He could come up behind me and slit my throat with a serrated kitchen knife at any moment if he wanted to.

"I will give you a hundred dollars if you give me the footage from yesterday," I say in an even, reasonable tone. "A thousand!" I quickly add even though there's no way I would do that, but what will she admit if she thinks that's a possibility? A woman who will charge ten dollars to let me pee will probably take a grand for the footage. That's probably what she recorded it for anyway. I expect her to start bargaining with me.

"Are you on dope?" she asks me.

"I saw the cameras."

"I don't know what the hell you're going on about. I don't even use a cell phone, and you think I know how to set up a camera?"

"You're a landlord. You can't act like some helpless old lady who doesn't know how to do anything," I say. She puts the cards down and curls her lip at me.

"Did I say helpless? Arty down at the bait shop takes care of all my computer stuff. He runs the website for me and deals with the reservations. All I do is clean the place, and Edgar fixes it up. We don't like all the interweb stuff, so whatever nonsense you're talking about, you can take up with him." She picks up the cards and shuffles one more time and smacks the deck down on the table in front of me.

"Pick one," she says, and I obey. I pull a card from the stack and turn it over. It's the grim reaper on a horse.

"Well, well, well," Alma says, smacking her gums and lighting another cigarette. She picks up a can of Diet Pepsi next to her and slurps, then sits back and folds her arms across her chest and waits for some response I guess I'm supposed to have.

"Well, well, what?" I ask.

"I told ya the other day already. As soon as I met ya, I saw it."

"Sure, sure. I'm cursed. What else ya got?"

"The death card."

"Oh," I say, feeling myself tremble a little, which is so stupid. I'm annoyed with myself and with the twenty bucks I'm spending for this bullshit.

"Yeah," she says.

"Well, that could mean a lot of things. Death of a career or a relationship. Doesn't it just mean change, not actual death?" I think I heard that somewhere before.

"Sure, lady. Whatever you say."

"How do you get business if you try to scare people?" I say, standing and pulling out the twenty I owe her and placing it on the table. She grabs my hand before I have a chance to pull away and looks me in the eye. I freeze, stunned by her action.

"People don't like the truth. That's not my fault. You should get out of here."

"I'm trying," I say and jerk my hand away.

"I mean the swamps. If I were you, I would leave now. Go home. Get out. Whatever is happening here . . . you're next."

A gagging sound behind us steals her attention, and she drops my gaze to turn around to observe one of her cats throwing up a furball in the threshold of the front door.

"Oh, Fuzz Lightyear, poor baby," she says, shoving the twenty in her bra and slamming the door behind her. I stand on the porch for a moment, her words like a thumb pressing on my breastbone. Of course she's batty, but the certainty in her expression, and all the shit that's happening . . . A little wave of nausea rises inside me. I take a deep breath and blow it out hard, trying to shake it all away.

I start to make my way back to the dock when I remember the shed. I know it's likely she can't even use a cell phone and the cameras aren't hers—fine. Maybe I need to hunt down some rando named Arty from the bait shop, but I at least can have a quick look while I'm here.

I quickly slip around the side of the cabin and climb past the overgrown bog grass. When I reach the shed, I poke one index finger at the half-open door to peer inside. It's not filled with electronics and my precious footage. There's a lawnmower and piles of junk like everywhere else. Shit. This was pointless.

I start sprinting back down toward the dock before they see me when I'm stopped by a voice.

"You're looking in the wrong place," a man's voice says, and I gasp, holding my chest in a bid to stave off a heart attack. I whip around to see Edgar sitting in a rocker on the front porch. He's no longer naked—wearing oversized Bart Simpson boxer shorts now—but he still has the cat with him, on his lap. He's chewing on sunflower seeds and spitting them out into the weeds.

"Sorry, I thought I left my . . ." I don't finish before he begins to laugh and shake his head.

"Would you like to feed Jonathan a teaspoon of milk?" he asks, holding a spoon up to the cat's mouth as it licks at the milk and purrs. I don't have any response to this. I can't even think of any possible response someone might have to this question.

"You shouldn't be out here alone like this," he says.

"Why? What do you think is going on? You think it's evil too?"

"I don't know. Could be, but you don't wanna end up like that other poor girl, do ya?"

"Elizabeth?"

"No," he says. "The one who's still alive."

"Emily? What do you know about it? Why would you say she's still alive?" I ask, my heart in my throat.

"'Cause I seen her."

"What? What do you mean? When?" Although this guy might be the most unreliable source in the world, what reason would he have to lie? What does he have to gain?

"Yesterday. Someone was dragging her screaming through the swamp across the way just there." He points across the water at a line of cabins.

"They forced her out of a boat, and somewhere—I don't know where—they took her from there. But she was alive."

"Someone? You saw someone drag her? Who— Did you see who it was?"

"It was just a dark figure. Death, it looked like."

"Jesus. Did you tell anyone? Did you tell the police for Christ's sake?" I ask, confused and panicked. Is this guy for real?

"The police don't care for me," he says, and I can see the big picture: *The Simpsons* boxers, the cats, the hoarding, the liquor. Would they have taken him seriously? Still. I can't believe what I'm hearing.

"You did nothing?" I ask.

He shrugs. "None of my business," he says.

"Where exactly did you see her?" I ask, and he stands and moves to the porch railing.

"Bog Island," he says and points to a small island across the swamp. My heart speeds up at this revelation. This is it. This is my moment. I can be the one to break the case, and they'll have to include me on camera, or in the credits at least. I won't tell the others until it's done. I will be the one to find Emily, the person to put all the pieces together. I look over to where he's pointing.

"You're positive," I ask.

"It was just light hair and skin I seen in a lightning flash, but it was her."

CHAPTER NINE

Macy

There's a low rumbling coming from the dark clouds as the Jeep bounces over the rough roads to town, and the smell of rain that hasn't fallen yet permeates the air. Lottie Tremblay has agreed to meet us at the revival tent rather than her house because she plans to pray and worship until Emily is found. Ethan drops me and Robert off before they head to the vigil, and as soon as we step out of the car, I can feel a shift in the energy—and it isn't good. There are twice as many people spilling out the sides of the tent, standing in the back and fanning themselves, holding hands up to God, or wiping tears. Panic. That's what's happening.

Robert raises his eyebrows at me and chucks the tripod over his shoulder as we make our way to the back of the tent where we stand by the refreshments table and wait for the sermon to end. He spots Lottie in the crowd and gives a nod in her direction. I see her. She's on her knees on the ground with her hands clasped together, her head resting on the folding chair in front of her. Her desperation is palpable and haunting.

Pastor Lawson is at the pulpit, charged up again, sweating and wiping the perspiration away with a handkerchief, shouting into the microphone.

"Banish from our town all spells, witchcraft, evil . . . In the name of the father. *Regna terrae, cantata deo, psallite cernunnos, regna terrae, cantata dea psallite aradia. Caeli deus, deus terrae, humiliter majestati gloriae tuae supplicamus ut ab omni infernalium spirituum potestate, laqueo, and deceptione nequitia omnis fallaciae, libera nos, dominates.*"

"Is he speaking in tongues?" Robert leans over and asks me. I shrug and gesture to his phone, and he covertly records the chaos. Some people stay seated and wail to the sky, others are on their knees with bowed heads, but most begin to form circles, holding hands and shouting over one another in a language that doesn't make sense—just a trill of sounds.

Lawson comes around and lays hands on different people, then punching a fist in the sky and chanting. He has one hand clasped around a man's head as the man shakes with his hands in the air. Lawson screams, "Heal this man with your Holy Ghost power!"

A few people fall to the ground and convulse as the people next to them drop to their side and lay hands on them, pleading to God, singing, crying. I've never seen anything like it before.

Robert mouths *What the fuck* at me. I have no response. I shake my head in disbelief. It all ends much more suddenly than I would have imagined when Lawson makes his way back up to the pulpit and asks if anyone would like to share their experience. Many folks walk down the aisle to speak in the mic, talking of how the Lord moved them and that they feel His presence here. A kid, no more than fifteen, takes the mic with trembling hands.

"There's just one name that can keep you out of hell. He spoke to me. There's just one name."

Everyone starts muttering, "Jesus." Most people are crying or lying on the floor.

"That's right, young man. Jesus!" Everyone cheers. It goes on like this for another hour or so until they break for fellowship. When the shouting and wailing turns into low chattering around the refreshments table and has spilled out onto the muddy lawn, I see Lottie is still on her knees on the mossy ground, unmoving. I gesture to Robert to cut the camera. I won't ask her if she wants to be recorded. Ethan would push it, which is part of the reason I insisted on taking this one. We have enough footage at this point. I just want to help—to get the whole story so we might start to piece it together.

I sit on the folding chair next to her, and Robert stays a row behind so she doesn't feel overwhelmed or like she's being interrogated.

She's clutching a photo of Emily, the one that's been all over the news and missing person signs. It's from the night she disappeared, a selfie she took with the girlfriend she met at the restaurant. She's wearing a blue print sundress, a huge smile on her face. The photo is worn and wrinkled. Lottie holds it to her heart and mumbles a constant stream of prayers.

"Lottie," I say softly, and she turns to me with bloodshot eyes and a grief so tangible it steals my breath.

"I'm Macy. Do you still want to talk? We can step out." She wearily stands. I take her hand to help her up. She's a thin-framed woman in a green sundress with skinned knees—from all the kneeling in the dirt, I suppose—and a wild mass of uncombed curly hair.

We follow her outside the tent and down the grassy embankment to the dock where there are camping chairs set up next to fishing gear someone left there. I sit across from her in one of the fold-up chairs, and Robert sits on the edge of the dock next to us, keeping a respectful distance.

"You'll put this on the computer so's people can see it and help find her?" she asks.

"Yes, the whole goal is to help find Emily," I say. Robert nods quietly in agreement.

"They're saying Elizabeth Brockton was found with her neck broken, spinning counterclockwise like some Devil sign. Says she was hanging high up in the trees, that there is no way someone could have put her there. It had to be . . . evil. They say she was involved in the occult. There's some dark entity after her—a demon maybe."

I was there, and she wasn't spinning. And someone certainly could have hoisted her up with a pulley rope—a noose. I saw it. The occult thing has no basis. It's just what people do. Make up more outrageous rumors in a desperate search for answers.

"I hadn't heard that" is all I say because I don't want to be combative in any way. That won't help anything right now.

"Pastor says it's evil among us, and I think he has to be right. Something was after Emily. Something happened. She stopped leaving the house, it scared her so bad. We could feel it in the house after that—a darkness."

"What happened?" I ask, exchanging a glance with Robert.

"Everyone knows Em was down on her luck. She's thirty-seven and had to come back to live at home. She wasn't proud of it. Got caught up in the meth and some bad friends. She needed a new start, so she left Lafayette when she lost her job a few months back, but she was sober now and really excited about going back to school to do hair. She's a good girl. Everyone has their problems; she was trying," she says and stops to dab her eye.

"Of course," I say, handing her a tissue from my bag.

"A couple weeks before she disappeared, she was home alone one night. It's just the two of us living in the house, and I was at bingo. She thought she heard something outside, so she paused the TV and went into the kitchen and looked out in the yard, and there was a hooded figure on the swings out back. We got a big stretch of woods behind the house." I feel a chill dance across my forearms.

"She goes to get her phone, and she doesn't call 911 right away, she told me. She thought maybe it was kids—teens or something—so she brings her phone back to the kitchen to look one more time, and at first she thinks it's gone. Maybe she imagined it. And then, out of nowhere, like a nightmare, there's a face in the window. The figure is standing, staring in at her. She said she screamed and ran, locking herself in the bathroom and calling the police. When she was on the phone with them, she stopped cold because she heard something that terrified her. The sound of the doggy door flap opening and closing. Duke passed a year ago, and there are no other pets in the house, but she heard it push open and swing shut. The man had crawled through the doggy door," she says, shuddering and blowing out a long breath. She looks to the sky a moment. "He was inside the house." Robert's eyes are wide, and we both wait for her to go on.

"She fled out the bathroom window and ran to the neighbors. We'll never know what happened. The police never found any leads, but she has been spooked ever since. She barely left the house for the last couple weeks. Then the first time she decides to go out—just to the Crawfish Hut to meet a friend for drinks—she's gone. Whatever that was, they got her."

I can't believe this information hasn't been circulating. We have rumors of the Devil hanging Elizabeth, but not a word that someone had broken into Emily's house while she was there. How did that not make the rumor mill?

"I say 'man,' but it wasn't a man," she says, as if she were reading my mind.

"What do you mean?"

"You think it was a woman? Could a man even fit through the dog door?" Robert asks, and she looks over at him with a furrowed brow as if seeing him there for the first time.

"Duke was a Saint Bernard. A man could have fit. We lock it at night for safety, but that's not what I mean. I mean I think it was something else. I don't know what to call it, but you'd understand if you went to my house. There's something in the air like fizzy electricity. Going inside feels like falling. I don't even want to be there. I'm staying at Sully's motel," she says, picking at the frayed fabric on the chair's armrest and shaking her head.

"Did Emily think it was a person—someone after her for any reason?" I don't want to say it was some guy she owed drug money to, but I have to wonder.

"She never wanted to talk about it. She only said she felt like she was being watched."

"Did she know Elizabeth?"

"All I know is that she was obsessed with her case. Elizabeth went missing some weeks before Emily did, and she was always talking about it. She would have theories and be online digging into the facts surrounding it. The police found a site she visited a lot, Satanic Ministries. I told them she must have been looking at it because she was researching Elizabeth. She must have learned something about that case that made her look there . . . but I'll never know if that's true or if she got caught up in something. It's easy for someone vulnerable, struggling with addiction to get manipulated, you know."

"I'm so sorry, Lottie. All this is . . . I can't imagine what you're going through. Is there anything you can share with our listeners that could help find her, help us understand—"

She cuts me off. "What if no one can help? What if there

is something really wrong with this place and we should all be running for our lives, getting out as fast as we can, and we're just like that frog, slowly boiling in a pot. We can't see what's right in front of us?"

Suddenly, a deafening crack of thunder explodes above us, and we all gasp. Lottie holds her heart. A few fat drops of rain start to fall, tapping the surface of the dock, a hiss of steam rising off the hot pavement of the parking lot across the way. We get up to run for the cover of the tent, but before we can move, a police car pulls up in front of Larry's Liquor and parks. Two officers get out and begin walking across the abandoned lot and over to the tent. We watch them, paralyzed.

An officer is chatting to a few members of the church by the refreshments table, and one of them points over to us. My stomach flips. This can't be good. The officers look to where the person is pointing and nods, then starts walking toward us. The one in front takes off his hat and holds it to his chest with his head slightly bowed, and we instantly know what that means.

Lottie collapses to the ground, wailing so loud the entire congregation is silent, and even the hiss of the rain is drowned out by her cries.

"No, no, no. My baby!"

CHAPTER TEN

Tasha

Bog Island is a tiny slip of land, mostly uninhabited because of the high alligator activity, especially during mating season. Thanks, Google. It's the end of mating season now, and the warning is still high for the area. Fuck me. What am I doing? Okay, be reasonable. They only attack if they feel threatened. They don't just swallow a kayak. That's ridiculous. Feeding time is early morning and evening, and everyone knows middle of the day is the safest time. This is not crazy. I am trying to save a life. Whether that's Emily's life, or maybe my own if I crack this case and wipe the floor with Macy and Ethan.

I will call the police and explain everything Edgar said in exactly one hour, I tell myself. Nothing will make or break the destiny of this situation in one hour. I might find her and save her, and if not—if Edgar is just an old bat, making shit up for sport—well then I'm no worse off than I started.

I've always been terrified of the swamps, their murky, hidden depths where anything can lurk, swarms of insects, parasites, disease, and now a potential murderer lurking in the shadows—and of course the possibility of getting eaten alive.

Why the fuck anyone would live here is beyond me. The only cabins on this godforsaken island belong to alligator hunters who stay here temporarily. As I glide up to the only rickety dock on the island, I'm greeted by nothing but silence.

I climb out of the kayak and listen for any signs of life. Thunder rumbles softly, and I know I don't have a lot of time before the sky opens up and I get poured on. *Petrichor.* The word flits across my mind because it means the smell of rain. Where did I read that? I don't remember, but the earthy, musky scent makes me want to curl up at home with tea and silence and not trying to find a kidnapped girl in the swamps. Anxiety courses through me, causing my hands to tremble ever so slightly, but I'm determined to find an answer.

"Emily!" I shout foolishly, only hearing my voice echo back at me. Crickets chirp in the reeds, and the birdsong from the treetops sounds almost like the ambient track you would play at night to help you fall asleep if this all wasn't such a nightmare.

I find a long stick and push muddy leaves and debris out of my path as I start around the perimeter and look up the muddy embankments to see if there are any clues someone is here. After walking for a few minutes, I see a cluster of cabins and decide to investigate. There are five in total—each small and built from logs, like fishing huts. I peer in the window of one, but it's mostly empty with the exception of a battered rug under two rocking chairs and some rifles piled in the corner. That seems safe.

The curtains are closed in the next cabin, so I bang on the door a couple times, knowing I won't get a response. Behind the cabin is a toolshed. The door is unlocked, and I quickly check inside, but it contains a bunch of tools and random equipment, nothing important.

If Edgar really saw someone dragging Emily onto this island, there are only a couple reasons that would make sense. Either someone—my stomach is in my throat as I even think it—brought her here to murder her, which wouldn't make much sense since she's been missing for weeks, or they brought her here to hold her captive. With no boat or kayak—no way to make it back to the mainland—she would be trapped. The hunters are gone until late summer, and it would be a secluded place to keep someone hostage or do whatever they want with her. If she tried to escape, she'd be shredded to bits by the gators. She'd have no chance.

It's most likely she was never here at all and this is the dumbest thing I've ever done. I walk to every cabin and tap on windows or try to peer inside, but it's eerily quiet. I think about giving up and heading back when I see something out of the corner of my eye. A bright shock of blue among the dull, brown vegetation all around. It's out of place, whatever it is.

My pulse quickens, and I stare over at it—about ten yards away—against some rocks on the shoreline. It could be litter, a Gatorade bottle, a beer can. But something in my gut tells me it's significant. I move in that direction, and when I'm standing over it, I still don't really know what I'm looking at. I take my stick and poke it, moving some mud off its surface. The realization almost knocks the wind out of me. I know exactly what it is.

I remember seeing it in the pictures and news clips. Emily on her last day, wearing a blue print sundress. It's a scrap of torn fabric. Powder blue with yellow daisies, exactly like the one she had on. Half of it is blood soaked. I kneel down on the muddy shore and stare at it, tears springing to my eyes.

"Oh God. This is really happening," I mutter. I hold my racing heart with my hand and look around as if there will be someone there to help me, but of course I'm the one who put myself in this situation. I take out my phone and start to dial for help but then pause a second because I see something so confusing and astonishing, the shock jolts me to my feet.

It's a pale, severed finger floating in the swamp water, caught in a cluster of cattails on the water's edge. A scream burbles up from my lungs, but I stop. I don't scream. I hold my breath and listen. There's something here. I'm not alone on this island.

I stay perfectly still and then I hear it again. Movement. A rustling in the swamp grass. Something is behind me.

I run. I don't look behind me or take a second to think, I just start running toward the cabins as fast as I can. My phone falls out of my hand, a small *thump* as it hits wet earth, but I can't stop. It's following me. There are footsteps, keeping pace, running after me. Oh my God. Something is coming after me. My lungs burn and my legs ache as I sprint, realizing there's nowhere to hide. I keep running, the tears streaming down my face, my breath coming in short gasps.

There was a toolshed behind one of the cabins that was open, I remember. It's my only hope. If it's an animal, I can probably escape it if I make it that far. I make a sharp turn to the right and run up the embankment to the cabin with the shed. When I turn, I see a flash of black against the trees. A dark shape with no discernible features coming right at me. I don't see a face. It doesn't even look human.

I think about all the rumors of evil circulating throughout the town. Suddenly, my fear of a rapist or serial killer turns to something else—thoughts of banshees and mothmen and demons. And the eight women who washed up in a northern lake with their faces missing. And the mysterious creature that drained the blood from dozens of sheep at night in Iowa. And the hiker found decapitated in his tent with no signs of entry or footprints around him. Stuff like that is out here. My mind reels and plays out every scenario as I scream until my lungs practically bleed, hoping the idiots across the swamp will hear me, but I already know they won't do anything, or they could have saved Emily.

I see the shed. I push myself the last few yards and collapse inside of it, slamming the door behind me, shakily feeling for a lock, doubting there will be one, but there is. I twist the deadbolt shut from the inside and fall to the floor, curling into a ball, staying as small and still as I can, watching the door, praying so hard that I'm safe. I lost track of how close it was. Maybe it didn't see me enter the shed. I cup my mouth with both hands so I don't make a sound.

Then the shattering of glass almost stops my heart. Behind me, the window is smashed, and before I can even move to run back out the door, it has me. Something covers my head, and I'm shrouded in blackness. I struggle against the hands holding me, but then I smell something chemical. It only takes a couple seconds before everything fades and I'm gone.

CHAPTER ELEVEN

Macy

A feeding frenzy. Ripped to bloody pieces by teeth tearing into flesh. The body parts that washed up on the mainland were examined and confirmed to be Emily's, the police said. But where's the rest of her? They scoured the water and some of the neighboring islands but couldn't find any more of her. The initial findings and probable cause of death were all over the press within minutes of the police breaking the news to Lottie, but that doesn't matter to the locals, especially the church revival folks. Everyone thinks it's demonic activity and that she was attacked by some satanic cult picking off women for sacrifices. At least those are the whispers I've heard over the last hour since it unfolded. The panic is even worse now.

Once Lottie goes with the police to identify her daughter's bracelet they found on her severed arm and do whatever they do in this kind of situation, Robert and I stand in the rain in stunned silence.

"Come on," he says, jogging over to a covered gazebo up the embankment. Once we're out of the rain, we squeeze out our wet hair and T-shirts and sit at a picnic table to wait for Max and Ethan to come back and get us. I think both of us are too exhausted and perhaps traumatized to get any more interviews. What else is there to say? Emily fell in the swamp, and either drowned or was eaten by alligators. Or both. I really want to go home now. The damp penetrates all the way to my bones, and all I want to do is bawl my eyes out for all of them—poor Emily and her mother. Elizabeth, Shane, and Lila—even though she did bite me.

Robert looks worse for the wear himself. He gets up and paces between the picnic tables, then pulls out the bag of sandwiches we brought, which are now a wet lump in his backpack, and slaps the soggy ball of bread on the table.

"Yum," I say like we could eat even if we wanted to. I push it away with a disgusted look and stare off across the knoll at the tent swaying and the mass of people inside moving together like a swarm of insects as they sing the haunting melody of an old hymn I remember from Sunday School. "*Are you washed in the blood? In the soul-cleansing blood of the Lamb?*"

"I don't know how you do it," he says.

"Do what?"

"This. That was the most depressing thing I've ever witnessed." He lets out a shaky sigh and rubs his eyes. "I think I'm gonna take off when we get back. Maybe see if there's a bus back to the city from town."

"Well, just so you know, I don't do this either, and I agree with you. We usually talk to dead people and Chupacabras and Sasquatches—not talk really, but shout for them to make themselves known," I say, mimicking the way Ethan always starts an episode. "This is fucked up, and I want out too. What else can we even do here?"

"Nothing," he says and then perches on the edge of one of the tables. He pulls the mental hospital pamphlet out of the netted front pocket of his backpack and leafs through it.

"I didn't see our friend Levi and his table today," he says as he skims the pages.

"Not even he could spin the blame of an alligator attack on escaped mental patients."

"Holy shit!" He holds the pamphlet away from him and then close to his face again as if he can't believe what he's seeing.

"What?"

"Coming soon," Robert reads. "Exclusive tours of Avalon Glade Lunatic Asylum. That's why that guy is trying to make the whole town think the hospital is this big, scary deal." He throws down the pamphlet on the table and stands. "This whole place is a ruse. Everyone is a crook preying on terrified people. Jesus Christ." I pick up the paper and look myself.

"Everyone's just trying to make a buck," I say. He sits, shaking his head and blowing the air out of his cheeks. The sounds of "Are You Washed in the Blood" turn into "The Old Rugged Cross" that the pouring rain tries desperately to drown out.

When Ethan and Max pull up, Robert and I hold our bags above our heads and sprint to the Jeep, leaping into the back seat. They've already heard about Emily. Everyone has.

"I think the cases are unrelated and Emily got very unlucky," I say, although nobody asked me.

"Well, we had an interesting experience," Max says as we drive through the rain. "Shane Brockton wasn't even at the vigil because it was discovered that his daughter, that crazy bat who stabbed Ethan—"

"Lila," I say.

"She had LSD in her system, and that's why she was acting so crazy. She was fucking drugged. They took him in for questioning," he says.

"What!" I exclaim. "That is . . . Wow."

"He must be the one behind all this. You said yourself it's always the husband," Ethan says, shaking his head.

"Behind Elizabeth. Probably. And I guess Emily was a tragic accident, it sounds like." There's a moment of charged silence and then Max smacks Ethan's arm, making him swerve a little.

"You gonna tell her?"

"Tell me what?" I ask, and there's another pause. Ethan pulls out his phone from his pocket and taps at the screen with his free hand as he navigates through the downpour with the other.

"We got it," he says, handing me his phone. On the screen is an email from Patty Hovland from Netflix. An offer. I read the letter with my mouth agape. Ethan and Max are hooting and hollering and punching the air.

"Congrats," Robert says in a measured tone.

"I can't believe it," I say, balancing a rush of contradicting emotions: excitement for this opportunity mixed with the grief of the situation. And maybe some guilt from the way we kept pushing into people's private pain.

"Let's get the hell out of here, then." If it were under any other circumstances, we might continue to cheer and turn the radio up and crack a beer from the cooler in the back even, but two people have just died, and it all feels wrong.

Max asks Ethan a bunch of questions about how this and that will work. Can he be an extra? Will they get to decide where the next episodes are? Or does Netflix have 'em by the balls now, etc. Mercifully, we reach the cabin, and I jump out the moment we pull to a stop. I can't get inside fast enough to start packing.

It only takes a minute to realize Tasha is gone, which is very unexpected. She doesn't have a car, and she didn't feel well. Where could she have possibly gone?

"Call her," I tell Max as he checks the two small rooms and the bathroom five more times before accepting that she's really not here. Robert goes to the porch and calls out for her. Nothing.

"How far could she go?" Ethan says.

Max tries to call her cell phone, and I see his expression change. "Goes right to voicemail. What the fuck?"

"Don't panic. She probably took a walk to get some air. Uber drivers don't come out here, so how else could she have left?" I say.

"That way," Robert says, pointing to the dock. "There used to be two kayaks, and now there's only one."

"There's a little convenience store across the swamp where Alma's place is. Maybe she needed something. We should probably just wait awhile before we overreact," Ethan says.

And so we wait. After an hour or two, Ethan cracks a couple beers and sits at the table with Max. They sip them and quietly scroll on their phones until Max gets up and starts pacing. He crushes the beer can in his hand and tries to shoot it into the garbage can against the wall. When he misses, it only fuels his agitation.

"We should go look for her," he says.

Robert, who has been putzing with a camera and tapping away at his phone, suddenly says, "Aha!" as the small TV on the battered console blooms to life. The interior of the cabin appears on the screen in black-and-white, like a security tape.

"What's that?" Ethan asks. There's an edge to his voice.

"I mounted a couple security cameras along with my EMF detector to see if we could capture any ghost activity in the cabin. I put one in the main area here and the porch, but it might be helpful to look at the footage to see if anything happened to Tasha," he says.

Ethan seems to go white. "Why would you do that?"

Max gets angry and talks over him. "What do you mean, if anything happened to her? She probably went across to that store, right? What could possibly have happened to her?"

"Nothing," Robert says calmly. "I just mean, get a better idea of where she might have gone, if she left in a hurry, whatever."

"I think we should go look for her now," Max says. "Forget sifting through hours of . . ."

He trails off as Robert starts fast-forwarding the footage. He stops, and we stand and stare at what is playing out on the screen. My jaw drops, and Max stands, watching, frozen as a statue.

It's Ethan and Tasha in the hot tub. They're kissing, on top of each other. Before we can even comprehend what's happening, Ethan lunges at Robert and grabs his phone and deletes whatever file Robert cast to the TV. It disappears from the screen and goes dark.

Max stares at Ethan with a bright red face, and his head looks like it could explode but is still immobilized.

I can barely process what I've just seen before Ethan is talking.

"There's a perfectly reasonable explanation for this. It was a game," Ethan starts to say, but then Max is up and launching himself at Ethan. He pushes Ethan in the chest so hard that he falls backward over the couch. Ethan tries to collect himself, scrambling back up to his feet, readying himself for another blow, but Max is already in the bedroom, shoving his things into a suitcase and screaming, "That's my wife! What the fuck, man! That's my wife!"

Robert is still standing with his hand out where his phone was before Ethan grabbed it, his mouth hanging open just like mine, watching this all unfold. Even though it feels like slow motion, it all happens so fast.

Max is out the door with his bag and a backpack slung over his shoulder, heading toward his Jeep. Robert runs after him.

"I'll talk him down. We'll look for Tasha," he says to me, but I don't move because I'm so stunned. I don't even know what to do with myself.

They drive off, and Ethan is there with pleading eyes. He takes my hand. My first reaction is to pull away from him, but he's gripping my hand hard. I give him a murderous look, and he quickly drops it.

"Hey, you know that was all for fun, right? You remember?"

I walk out the screen door, completely numb, sit on one of the rocking chairs, and try to catch my breath. He comes and kneels on the floor in front of me.

"Please say you remember, Mace."

"Remember what?"

"Tell me you weren't sleepwalking."

"What the fuck are you talking about?" I ask, forcing myself not to cry, not to rip all his hair out in clumps and beat him with my fists right now.

"You were there, in the hot tub. We were playing stupid games, truth or dare, or whatever, and we were really drunk. You told us to make out—that it would be funny. I said it's not a good idea, but you practically forced it. It was just for a second and then that was it. You don't remember?" he says.

"I wasn't—" I stop. Was I?

"We were all really hammered," he says. "I never thought you were having an episode or that you wouldn't remember. Still, it shouldn't have happened."

I think about how drunk and hungover Tasha was, which was so unlike her, and how Ethan and I fought about him flirting with Tasha before I went to bed. Could I have only been partly conscious? Could I have been that drunk? Or maybe I was asleep for part of it, and that's why I got mad at him for flirting. It would make sense, when I think about how the night played out, but I honestly don't know.

No matter whether I was a part of this or not, I can't look at him right now. Thunder rumbles low and soft in the distance, and clouds are pushing in.

"Can you please leave me alone right now?" I say.

"Mace, it was just a stupid drunk night."

"Then why did you delete the footage from his phone?"

"I don't know; it was just a reaction. Wouldn't you be pissed if you were secretly recorded? You were just outside of the frame. You were standing there." He points to a place across the deck by the cooler that the camera didn't capture. "You were getting a drink and laughing at the whole thing," he says. "You gotta remember."

"Okay," I say. "I need some space." He always gives me my space when I ask for it, so he stands and kisses me on the cheek.

"I'll go and help look for her," he says.

"How?" I ask, because the Jeep is gone. He points to the small boat at the dock.

"I'll go to the islands around us and look for the kayak, ask if anyone saw her. I'll talk to Alma."

"Take the kayak," I say, and he doesn't ask why. Probably because he's walking on eggshells and wouldn't dare try to combat me on anything right now. He picks up an oar and gets in, pushing away from the shore. I know a storm is coming, and if these roads get washed out, I need a plan B. A boat with a motor, not a fucking kayak. I want out now, but we have to find Tasha first. Something's not right. I can feel it.

An hour goes by, and nobody comes back to the cabin. Dusk is setting in, a light rain starts to fall, and I'm starting to wonder if something's happened. Max won't pick up. I realize I don't actually have Robert's number—why would I? And Ethan's phone goes right to voicemail. I want out. Now.

The low-country boat is still tethered to the dock. Should I take it before it gets too dark? Where would I go though? We're on the mainland, and it's too far and wet to walk to town—to civilization. If I take the boat to the tiny islands, I'm even more deserted though. I would be going the wrong way.

They'll come back, I tell myself, but night is falling fast, and it feels like the Rapture is coming. Nobody is answering. Everyone is gone. I'm totally alone here.

I stand inside the screen door for what seems like an eternity, watching for any movement, and then my heart almost leaps from my chest. The Jeep is back! I run to the bedroom, slip into flip-flops, and grab my phone and my packed bag, ready to get the fuck out of here. But as I go to whip open the screen door, there is a face staring at me from the other side of it. It's not Max's or Robert's. It's Shane Brockton's. I jolt backward, holding my chest.

"What are you— I thought you were arrested. What are you doing here?" I say, terrified, putting together that he is probably a cold-blooded killer, and whatever reason he has for being here can't be good. I look behind him and see a small, ghostly pale face peering out from the passenger's seat of his truck. Lila.

He opens the door, and I stumble backward as he pushes his way in, practically falling over the crap that's on the main room floor—cameras, bags, mics. I stop when I literally have my back up against a wall.

"I was let go because, of course, they have nothing to go on. And only a psychopath drugs a kid, and that ain't me. Is it you?"

"What?!" I snap. I'm in disbelief he would be here at all, let alone accusing me of something like this.

"I ain't gonna let Lila hear any of this, so you're lucky. But just know . . . I'm onto you."

"What the fuck are you talking about?" I move forward a little, confident now that he doesn't plan to kill me in front of his daughter.

"All the shit that's gone down; it only started after you people showed up. You better start watching your back because you won't get away with it," he says. I shakily pull out my phone to call the police on this delusional nutcase, but in one swift move, he plucks the phone from my hand and starts marching toward the front door, the screen door slamming behind him. From the front porch, he hurls my phone into the swamp water. It's immediately swallowed by the blackness.

"What the fuck is wrong with you?!"

"Ask yourself that question. You mess with my kid, you got a lot bigger problems than your phone, lady."

I stand there completely dumbfounded. Even though I feel like I must be sobbing, there are no tears, just utter shock.

"Are you insane? You think I—we came here because of the disappearances. The trouble did not start with us. We came here to get to the bottom of what's happening."

"Lila was drugged the night you people showed up to my house pretending to want to help. I know I didn't do it, so where does that leave us? I started looking into you and your channel—exploiting ugly situations and tragedies for your own pocketbook. I already know the kind of people you are."

"It's just a ghost hunting show. It's not that serious," I start to say, but he talks over me.

"You came down here seven weeks ago, end of April, to film some stupid thing at the Magnolia Plantation. The same day Elizabeth disappeared. Your videos online are time-stamped. You didn't think someone would eventually put that together?" he says, looking back at Lila and trying to keep his fury controlled.

"What?" is all I can manage because I'm so confused by what he's saying.

"April twenty-seventh. You were in town," he says, and I feel a shock bolt through me. I didn't hear about Elizabeth's disappearance until a couple of weeks later, and I never put that timing together, but it's true.

"You think we had something to do with Elizabeth? You're coming here to tell me we're murderers and poisoned a child. That's what you're saying to me right now?" I snap at him.

"That's exactly what I'm saying to you." He looks back at the truck to his daughter and then at me.

"If the law don't get you, I will. That's a promise." He turns and goes to his truck, screeching out of the little clearing in a cloud of exhaust and dust, and speeds off.

I'm left breathless by the encounter, my heart hammering. I stand on the porch with only the sounds of crickets and cicadas, and I feel like I could go crazy. I don't even know where to focus my panic. I could panic over now being stranded without a phone on top of the rest of it, but all I can think of are his words. *You came down here seven weeks ago . . . The same day Elizabeth disappeared.* I think of Ethan pleading with me to remember. Was I up last night; did I do something I have no recollection of? Jesus. My heart plummets to my stomach, and my hands tremble.

A week later, we came down to try to scout things out—see if we could talk to Shane and line up some interviews, and to see if the story was worth pursuing, and then Emily disappeared. Then we all agreed it was worth getting a small crew and coming down for a while for a bigger story. That means I was in town when Emily was killed too. Oh my God.

I think of all the crazy shit I've done sleepwalking—I went swimming in the middle of the night in the lake behind our house as a kid. Another night, the neighbors across the way found me in their yard. I once stood over Ethan while he was asleep, holding a pair of scissors and staring at him with a wild look in my eyes. He slept in the guest room with the door locked for a week after that. I even pulled my pants down and peed on the coffee table in the living room, waking up right in the middle of doing it. I have probably done so much that I don't remember.

What might I be capable of? What if I crawl through dog doors at night or slit someone's throat? My mind reels. What if I can't trust myself at all, and I'm the monster?

Just then, a spine-chilling sound pierces the air. It's a scream in the distance—across the swamp.

"No! Help me!" The panic and desperation in the voice is palpable.

It's Tasha. I run inside, grab the shotgun from where it leans against a wall behind the door, and sprint as fast as I can down to the dock and untether the boat. It's my only way to get to her.

CHAPTER TWELVE

Tasha

When I wake up, I'm still in the shed. My feet are duct-taped together, and so are my hands. I'm lying on the muddy floor, half wedged under a tool bench. My head is heavy and fuzzy as I push myself up from the floor to a sitting position. The inside of the shed is dark, just the faint glow of dusk penetrating through the broken window, and it takes only a second before sheer panic rises up inside me. I try to swallow it down, knowing that if I have any chance of surviving, I need to keep calm and think quickly. There's no time for falling apart. I don't have the luxury.

I look down at my hands and realize that it might be the first time all my garbage doomscrolling on social media has actually come in handy in real life. I didn't understand then how there would be enough people finding themselves in this situation to need such a video, but there are countless videos about how to escape from restraints like zip ties. And duct tape. A former FBI agent made a TikTok saying people all over the world are kidnapped using duct tape. It's one of the easiest restraints to get out of, but most people would have no idea how. I try to quiet the panic in my mind long enough to remember the steps. Hold your hands high above your head, and pull your wrists apart as you pull your hands down as fast as you can. At a certain angle, they'll snap off like nothing. It takes me a few tries, but on the fourth try, the duct tape snaps, and I'm free. I'm stunned that it was that easy.

I rummage around in the near dark, trying to find something I can cut the tape on my ankles with. There's no trick to get out of that. The first thing I feel is a scattering of nails on the floor, so I grab one and pick at the edge of the tape until it starts to fray and peel away. When the slit is big enough, I try tearing the rest of the tape, but I'm shaking so violently, it's hard to keep my hands steady enough to do it.

Once I finally do free myself, I can feel the tears forming, and I have to try hard to steady my breath and stay focused. I don't know where the hooded figure is. Are they watching? Waiting outside the cabin to kill me and feed me to the alligators the minute I step outside? I hold very still and listen. There is only wind through the swamp reeds and frogs croaking and the distant song of a mockingbird in the evening air.

I have to make my move even if someone is lying in wait to slit my throat too. It's my only chance. I slowly open the door, pause for a second, and run as hard as I can back down to the small dock where my kayak is still pulled up on the muddy bank, ready to take me to safety. A cry escapes from my lips when I look at the bottom of the kayak and see that the plugs have been removed and are nowhere in sight. Without those plugs, the kayak will sink in a matter of seconds.

I look out into the water and see scaly heads and protruding eyes right in front of me. There would be no surviving if I tried swimming, even though I can practically see our cabin across the way. The distance is easily swimmable, and Alma's island is just to the west of that and even closer. I could practically spit on them. How can I be so completely trapped when safety is so close? I don't know whether to scream because what if the figure hears and comes back? Where did they even go? But since there is no other boat on this tiny slip of land, I know nobody else is here.

I run back to the shed and look around for some kind of weapon. Something like hope washes over me when my hand brushes against a hammer by the door. The cabin next to the shed is locked up, but I need to get in. There has to be something I can find to plug up those holes in the kayak and get out of here. There has to be. Duct tape is all I need, but I'm guessing the figure was probably smart enough not to leave that where I could find it, if he took the time to pull the plugs just in case I got loose.

I walk around the outside of the little hunting cabin and look for the best window to smash. One that's not right in front, so if he comes back, he might not see it right away or notice it at all. When I locate a more hidden window, I don't hesitate. I smash the shit out of the glass with all my might and then pick at the glass around the edges so I can shimmy my way in. I have to run back over to the shed and grab a few oil rags to lay over the window frame so I don't get shredded to bits when I push myself in.

Once I hoist myself up and through, I fall onto the floor beneath the windowsill, sit up, and blink, taking in the horror around me. I have to clasp my mouth closed to hold in my screams. Oh my God. This can't be real.

It's a small two-room cabin. Just a main area and a kitchenette and a short hall leading to the back. The entire main room is covered in sheets of plastic. Each wall is draped with taped-up plastic sheaths that stretch from floor to ceiling. Even the ceiling is covered with one giant square of plastic, and there's a sheet on the floor as well. There is only a white folding table in the middle, also covered in plastic, and a medical bag of sharp tools I can't even bring myself to look at any closer. There's a pile of towels and plastic bags on the floor against a wall and a five-gallon bucket. I tell myself not to look at what's inside that bucket, but I have to. I nearly vomit at the sight. It's filled with blood. There is only one reason a room would be shrouded in plastic from top to bottom.

This is a kill room.

I stand paralyzed in fear. I can't even scream. But I feel like I'll hyperventilate if I try holding down my sobs any longer. I keep swallowing them as the surges of fear and adrenaline keep me moving, thinking, but I don't know what to do next.

I push the hanging plastic aside and walk into the small kitchenette so I can exit the back door. I need something heavy duty to plug the holes in the wood. Something with no chance of leaking. I think of shoving sheeted plastic in the holes, but I also think about water seeping around the sides and me sinking to my bloody death. I need Flex fucking Tape or I don't know. People use boats to get here. Someone must have something to repair a leak. I have to break into another cabin and look.

As I push the plastic out of my face, the kitchenette looks incongruous to the rest of the horror show inside. It's a happy little space with a ceramic frog for a sponge holder, a couple fake plants, a little plaque on the wall that says bless this mess, and a small basket next to the back door for mail and keys. I'm so confused, I'm spinning. It looks like someone's mother lives here—until someone turned her home into an execution chamber. My God. I step out the back door to breathe and think about what to do next—what I can use to get the kayak to float—when something catches my eye.

Two mid-century, mint green clamshell chairs are on a round outdoor rug with a small metal table between them, on top of which is a very recently opened beer, still sweating in the Louisiana heat. My first thought is wildly optimistic, that someone is here who can help me. My second, more probable, thought is that it's my abductor's beverage.

That's when I notice a small hand-carved wooden sign attached to the side of the cabin. THE GOFFS. I gasp at the sight of it and stumble backward. No, it can't be. Macy and Ethan Goff. Is this their cabin? Are they somehow involved in all this? My mind spins trying to make sense of it all.

I think of all the drinks nights with them and that trip to Cabo years ago, the dinner parties, the movie nights.

What the fuck did I miss? There's no way. But what other explanation is there? My mind plays back every moment I can recall that might make this make sense—dumb drunk fights they've had or body language or looks exchanged that should have tipped me off. But nothing comes to mind. Sure, we didn't always get along, but I still considered them friends. Normal people. Not . . . murderers. This would take a total narcissistic psychopath to pull off. How could I have missed that?

Before I even have a chance to try to get control of my swirling thoughts, I hear something. The unmistakable sound of oars splashing in water and something being pulled up through the mud. *Chhhh-chhh*. The sound of the dragging is the most terrifying noise I've ever heard. I run.

I run to the farthest cabin, but the island is so small, you can easily see all the way across it. It's just a small sandbar really with trees and a handful of cabins. There is absolutely nowhere to run. I smash the window of another cabin, instantly regretting my panicked move because they probably heard it. The word *they* catches in my mind. God, what if it's both of them working together? But why? Maybe I should have buried myself in brush or muddy leaves instead, but somehow I feel safer inside a building than out in the open.

I quickly think of a different strategy. If I take the hammer and hide inside this cabin, maybe I can get them first when they come sniffing me out. As I'm pushing through the broken window, I shred my shirt and the skin on my chest, but the adrenaline coursing through me prevents me from feeling any pain in that moment.

I shimmy inside and scan the room. This cabin is very different—a normal person's place with a flannel couch and rocker-recliner in the main area. Same layout with the kitchenette, but slightly bigger with room for a tiny bedroom to the side. I fall to the ground and push myself underneath the bed, holding the hammer so tightly in my hands, my knuckles feel like they're bleeding.

It's very near dark now. Maybe they won't see the broken window. Then something dawns on me—something so terrifying that I emotionally give up and begin sobbing in the fetal position under the bed.

The rain has recently stopped, and my footprints would easily track every move I've made. They'll find me in minutes. And they do.

The rest swirls together in a haze—an explosion of stars behind my eyes, a slow-motion night terror. Muddy boots approach, I hold the hammer with both hands, and it's hard to get leverage in my position but I just strike, praying to make contact. Then I hear a cracking of bone, but maybe I missed and hit the bed frame. I'm pulled out by my hair, swinging my arms, screaming, and dragged outside into the darkness where I let out a bloodcurdling scream. "No! Help me!"

CHAPTER THIRTEEN

Macy

There are only two islands across the way: Bog Island and Tupelo. I know exactly where the scream came from, and as I make my way across the murky water in the darkness, I hope I'm not too late. There are no lights on Bog Island, so I can only find my way by the moonlight, which has pushed through the storm clouds, and a flashlight I found in the cabin that's starting to peter out.

When I pull up to the dock, I see two kayaks lying on the shore and muddy footprints leading up the embankment. I see a small light on in a shed about ten yards away, and I clutch my gun and rush over to it, breathless and unsure what I'll find. I've been here before. Ethan's father has kept a hunting cabin on this island since he was a kid, and before his father passed away, they used to go gator hunting here in the fall. He showed it to me last time we were here covering Magnolia Plantation, and that's how we found the cabin we're staying in—word of mouth from his time spent in the area. The place is inherently creepy, which makes sense since it only exists for people to come and kill other creatures.

I could have never prepared myself for what I see next. Tasha, her mouth duct-taped, is tied with vinyl rope to a metal folding chair in the center of the cluttered shed. Her feet are bound. Tears are streaming down her cheeks. She startles when she sees me, and a look of fear flashes across her eyes when she sees the gun in my hands. She starts pushing herself backward and trying to scream beneath the tape, like she's afraid of me. I pull it off, and she is silent, staring at me.

"What the fuck?"

"Are you with him?" she says, which makes no fucking sense.

"What?"

"Are you in on this with him?"

"With who? What are you talking about?" And then she changes tack.

"Hurry. Get me loose. Hurry! It's him," she whispers.

"You have to start making sense," I say, petrified and shaking, holding the gun toward the door opening and keeping my back to the wall. "What the fuck is happening?!" I yell.

"Shh. He's still here. He'll hear you. You have to get me out of here. He's coming back. He's going to kill me."

"Who? Who are you talking about?"

"He killed Elizabeth. He told me. She was dying anyway, he said." Tasha starts crying so hard I can barely understand her between sobs. "He said he did her a service—a mercy. He did it so he could be the one to solve the case and the channel would get the TV deal."

"Are you talking about Ethan? What? Tasha that's—"

"Yes, Ethan! He only admitted to this stuff because he's gonna kill me, Mace. I found out too much and now . . . We have to hurry," she says. I can't control the trembling of my hands as I desperately search for anything to cut her loose.

"Please!"

"I'm trying." I start sobbing too now, trying to understand what's happening. I feel lightheaded, and it's a struggle to breathe.

"The kid—that little girl—he gave her those cookies that night. He wanted footage. He wanted her to freak out, to look possessed, for the videos. The attack, when someone grabbed you at the mental hospital. He staged that. When we cleared the place, he did find a couple squatters and paid them to attack you so he could get it on camera. You don't understand what he's capable of," she says, trying to wriggle out of the restraints.

"I saw the video of you two in the hot tub. You were trying to sleep with him. How can I even trust anything you're saying?"

"I think he drugged me too. I didn't drink that much, and I've never felt that out of it before. I—"

We both stop dead as we hear footsteps approaching the shed.

"No," she whimpers, and I hold up the shotgun and point it at the door. When Ethan steps in, he halts in a stunned silence and looks at me. I keep the gun aimed at his chest. Fear registers on his face, but then he smiles.

"Mace, what are you doing here?" he asks, so calmly it takes my breath away. There is no way for my mind to process what Tasha told me.

"You . . . This was all you? Tell me you didn't kill anyone. That's—that's crazy."

"The proof is in that cabin," Tasha says, and he backhands her so hard, it looked like her neck would snap. She cries out, and blood seeps from her nose. That's the moment I know that what Tasha told me was the truth. The truth about him. Even a second ago I might believe she had it all wrong—a string of bad luck and misunderstandings—but there was nothing but blackness behind his eyes when he smacked her.

There must be all the evidence we'd need to ruin his life in that cabin, or he wouldn't have let himself snap.

He would have denied it all—called her crazy. But he didn't.

"You really fucked this up, Macy. Goddamnit! Both of you. We could have had it made. Netflix was tossing around a half-million dollar advance, and you literally just ruined it. You're gonna have to be with me on this, Mace. You have to."

"I don't . . . understand. You killed Elizabeth? That's—No. Oh my God. And what about Emily?"

"Listen. We can still do this. What you have to understand is that this isn't what it seems, okay? I'm not some monster. Elizabeth was already dying. She had weeks left. So that shouldn't really count, but I was never trying to kill anyone. They both got themselves killed. I was only going to take Elizabeth for a few days, and we would find her and be the heroes. That was the original plan. But she pulled my mask off the first night, and what was I supposed to do? She saw who I was, and I had no choice. And Emily wasn't my fault. She got obsessed with Elizabeth's case—some junkie with nothing better to do—and started snooping around. I brought her to the shed behind our cabin, but she ran. She almost got away, so I had to keep her here on the island so I could think—just until we could solve the case and I could cover my tracks a little better. She's the idiot who tried to swim to safety."

"She was in the shed. Behind our cabin while we were there?" I ask, vomit rising in my esophagus. The boarded up cabin Alma told us to leave alone. Jesus.

"When you went to sleep that first night, I had to move her so she wouldn't run again. Macy, I don't see what the problem is here. That was seriously ingenious of me. She would have been fine if she didn't freak out and try to escape."

"Oh my God," I mutter, my heart beating in my throat, my arms tingling, and my stomach about to betray me.

"It can all be okay. I did this for you. For us. It's sad that all this had to happen, but it's their own goddamn fault. Then this moron"—he gestures at Tasha—"has to come fuck it up even further. I know it sounds . . . wild, babe, like, I know that, okay, but we can still make all our dreams come true. We can be famous. The money is right there. Don't give that up for this bitch," he says. I look over to Tasha, whose eyes are wide with fear.

"How is she even here? How did you know she'd be here? I don't understand," I ask, still trying to put all the pieces together.

"I ran into Alma and Edgar at the vigil. He said Tasha paid them a visit and that she was headed over to Bog Island to poke around for clues. I knew we were screwed, so I took the Jeep and left Max for an hour. I went back to the cabin and took the kayak and knew I'd fucking find her, and here she was, like Edgar said. I have only done what was necessary every step of the way. For us. I love you. Look at what our life could be, Mace. Come oooon."

"Who are you?" I say, my mind spinning and unable to come up with any other words.

"Let's not be dramatic. Look," he says, holding his hands up in a surrender position. "I'll let her go. By the time she figures out how to get help, I can have that cabin spotless, untraceable. She'll sound crazy. There's no other proof. I made sure of that. Nobody will believe the jealous best friend who never got her life together and wishes she was you." I see Tasha wince, but then he pulls out a pocketknife, and to my surprise, cuts her loose.

"See?"

"He's lying. He's gonna hurt you, Macy. He'll never let you walk out of this. Shoot him!" Then I see Ethan smile and flick his blade open. Tasha is running at me to get control of the gun, and I scream until my throat feels like it's bleeding, and I close my eyes and I shoot.

CHAPTER FOURTEEN

Tasha

Ethan wails as he falls to the ground with a hard smack. He's struck in the leg, but it doesn't stop him. Macy drops the gun and stumbles backward, looking at her own hands and screaming like she's killed him or something. He swings an arm over his head from the place where he's lying on the floor and tries to grab it, but I get to it first. He scrambles to his feet, grabbing his leg in pain.

I back up out of the shed, but I'm too slow, and he swipes the open blade at me, catching my arm. I feel the warm blood seep through my shirt and bloom red against the pale pink fabric. I make the mistake of momentarily looking down in horror, and that's when he makes a move for the gun. I manage to elbow him in the neck and get outside the shed, keeping control of the gun. I point it at his face, and he holds up his hands again, this time laughing, thinking I don't have it in me.

I don't even hesitate. I take a shot. The blast jolts me back, and the swamp goes quiet for a moment. I missed, but he's scared now. He knows I can pull the trigger if it really comes to that.

"I didn't want to do this," he says. Macy is still crying with hiccupped sobs. "I never wanted to involve you, Mace, but just know that nobody spends this many weeks and months plotting something like this out without thinking of every turn. That bloody rag we cleaned up with when you crushed the glass while you were sleepwalking? It's in a five-gallon bucket with your name all over it. Plus a headband Emily was wearing . . . Did you have a fight with her, snap? It's all in a cabin you knew existed. Each detail of this was well crafted, and that's just one small line item on my list. Every step of the way, it will look like you are the perpetrator. Emily's phone is even in your gym bag back at our condo at home. Don't think I didn't plan it to the letter."

"Jesus Christ," I whisper. Macy's sitting in the mud, shaking.

"So you coming?" he says, but she doesn't move.

"Okay, then." He looks to me. "You ain't a killer. A slut, maybe, not a killer." He turns and starts to run, limping, trying to make it to the kayaks. I follow him with the gun still pointing at him. Macy gets up and is a step behind me.

He gets into the kayak and with all the confidence in the world that I won't shoot, and he paddles away. We're not in immediate danger if he flees, so I don't shoot. I have to believe there is some justice, that the truth will come out and there's no way he'll get away with this. And I really don't want to have to live the rest of my life with the knowledge that I killed someone.

Suddenly, Ethan's scream pierces through the darkness. Macy aims her flashlight out to the swamp a few yards in front of us. Ethan is flailing in the water, his screams becoming garbles.

I look down to see the kayak left on the shore has all its plugs. He took the wrong one.

We watch helplessly as he's crushed and torn apart in the black, black swamp water.

EPILOGUE

One Year Later

Macy

When we finish filming the last episode of *Ghost Patrol* for the Netflix series, it's Tasha who's in front of the camera. I have opted to stay in a producer role and do some of the writing. It's where I preferred to be all along. Tasha and I don't have quite the same vibe—the believer and the skeptic hashing it out—but it doesn't matter because of the "ripped from the headlines" spin they're giving the show. It will sell simply because of what actually happened, and Tasha does a good job.

She sits there enrobed in the bright lights and cameras, and gives her closing lines like a natural.

"We can't close this out without me telling you that Alma Braithwaite is the real deal. She called it. She saw me dying. I almost did. She saw that, and it's only a twist of fate that saved me from what she predicted. If you go and see her, just be prepared for the truth."

Then it's a wrap. I don't know if that little plug is a blessing or a curse for Alma and Edgar—turning them into a tourist attraction—but I have a feeling she'll handle it just fine.

Max and Robert have taken positions on sound and lights and are over the moon. Well, as much as anyone can be after what we've been through. All of us are changed by what happened in the swamp. There are moments of laughter following a joke—an attempt to get back to normal—but the grief that rests just underneath the surface is always there. All the things we don't say aloud and all the press and comments left online are invasive. We don't read them anymore.

I don't know if going ahead with a show was the right thing, but it gets the truth out there, it's financial security, and it's something to focus on during the days I think I'll lose my mind still trying to come to terms with all that's happened. Perhaps I should have moved away to a little town where nobody has heard of me. But everyone has heard of me now. And everyone has an opinion. Despite the support of most people, there are always . . . the others.

There's no way she didn't know. She's the wife, of course she knew. She was just as obsessed with fame as him. She's a murderer who got away with it. If I ever see that bitch, I'd shred her to bits just the way she did to that poor girl. She should be in prison. I'll kill her myself.

"Don't read the comments section; don't open emails," I whisper to myself on a daily basis. I didn't prepare for a life where thousands of people—millions, maybe—hate me and want me dead. The scandal and controversy are hot for a TV show, but it's already too much, and I fear when it airs, I'll have ruined my life. *She's just as guilty. She should be hanged from a tree too. She should rot in hell.* The comments never stop. The threats show up every day. I had to close down all my social media.

When our house sold, I moved to Los Angeles to a small studio until I figure out what's next. I had to find a building with high security, a twenty-four-hour guard at the door. I stay anonymous as much as I can. I wear a ball cap around when I go out, and I constantly look over my shoulder. This is my life now. This is what he did it all for.

Max startles me out of my thoughts. As everyone gathers their things, he reminds me that we're meeting at a pub across town for drinks. Tasha comes and puts her arm around me.

"Only if you're up for it," she says.

"'Course," I say, but I would rather go home and be alone. That's the only place I feel safe. But I'm thankful for my renewed friendship with Tasha in the aftermath of everything. She's kept me afloat, kept me breathing, when all I want to do sometimes is give up.

When I reach my car in the parking lot, I see someone has left a note on the windshield. I open it. There's a message scrawled in red marker.

Killer.

ACKNOWLEDGMENTS

There are so many people that make a book come together and there are countless folks to credit who have put so much hard work into making this happen. A special thank you to the best agent in the world, Sharon Bowers, and to Stephanie Beard at Podium who offered to let me be even weirder than usual in the form of a novella and believed in my ability to lean a bit more horror and bizarre which was so much fun to do.

Thank you to my incredible editor, Erin McClary who is truly collaborative and totally gets me.

Thank you to Katherine Odom-Tomchin at Folio and the whole team at Podium who have been of great encouragement and support: Nicole Passage, Laura Vorhees, Taylor Bryon. Eloise Davenport, Mitch Raynes, Keara Wood, and designer Elizabeth Yaffe, along with illustrator M.S. Corley, and many more.

Of course, thank you to my ever-supportive family, especially my mother, Dianna Nova, and my husband and biggest fan, Mark Glass.

ABOUT THE AUTHOR

Seraphina Nova Glass is a bestselling author, an award-winning playwright, and an assistant professor of instruction and playwright-in-residence at the University of Texas at Arlington, where she teaches film studies and playwriting. She holds a Master of Fine Arts degree in dramatic writing from Smith College and a second MFA in directing from the University of Idaho.

Her novel *On a Quiet Street* was nominated for an Edgar Award and was featured in the *New York Times*, the *Boston Globe*, and *Bustle*. Glass is a proud dog mom and loves to travel the world with her husband. She resides in Dallas, Texas.